Divide and Take

J. Collin

To Cindy, Luci, Ryland, and Edi

Chapter 1

The volume was more than a little high on the television. Larry Bachmann, an evangelical preacher, was holding his audience captive on the Sunday church program. He was talking about the harm of engaging in gay "activities" and trying to link dropping testosterone levels to an increase in gay men. The Evangelical stood in front of hundreds of people and a camera, leading the sinners out of darkness and making parishioners believe they were saved. In a strong and angry voice Bachmann asserted homosexuality is indeed a sin. The good news Larry offered was that being gay is one hundred percent curable. The only requirement was just to trust God and stop doing things simply meant to give pleasure. Bachmann was dressed in what I am guessing was an expensive suit talking about feeling close to God. He would raise his voice sometimes for dramatic effect, creating a backdrop of good and evil, for which there was no gray area. There was only an eternal struggle between God and the devil.

On the sofa next to me sat Jill, my partner. Without even looking up from her magazine she took the remote control out of my hand and shut the TV off. "You don't want to be watching that."

I laughed. "No, really, I was watching that."

"Ok, this is just stupid."

"It's entertaining," I said with a grin.

"Those people are hurtful and ignorant," Jill replied.

"I'm not defending them Jill, but I doubt their goal is just specifically to hurt us." I wasn't sure why I was defending the preacher; perhaps it was because Jill always had such a strong conviction she was right about everything. "They're just trying to make the world better the best way they know how."

Jill was getting a little peeved with me. "I'm not sure I can sit on the fence with this issue Sarah, especially when this jack-off is calling me immoral."

"Alright," I said getting a little tired of the argument.

"Yes, maybe, if they did not force their views on others. They gather in their churches and decide what is right and wrong for the world. Those people have lobbyists in Congress and at the state level, just to make sure we don't have the same rights as they do."

"I am not saying what they do is not sick and just plain weird, but do you really think calling them stupid or telling them they are wrong is just going to change their minds?"

Jill looked up and changed the subject, "Speaking of the moral majority, you should tell your parents about us."

"Jill," I said with a sigh, "I have to work."

"Sarah," Jill replied. She looked at me as though she really felt that today would be the day I would suddenly jump out of my closet.

"Not going to happen."

Jill looked at me with a critical smile. "How long have we been together?"

"Five years," I said smiling.

"And how many times have you met my family?"

"You're looking at the situation through your eyes, not mine. Things are different with your family."

"You sleep at my house all the time, but you have your own house. This isn't really a commitment."

I put my hands on Jill's shoulders "I'm committed to you, Jill."

"Do you love me?" she asked challenging me.

"Of course I love you! I can't believe you would even have to ask that." I said giving Jill a kiss.

"Then prove it. We should make some sort of a formal commitment and that commitment should involve our families."

"Yeah," I said with an almost sarcastic tone.

"Sarah, I would like your family to see me as more than the girl you hang out with in Grand Rapids. What if something happened to you? I couldn't just go to your family after something happened and tell them about us."

"I have to get to the store, babe." I leaned over and kissed Jill.

"Just think about it Sarah," she said.

"Yes dear," I replied in an exhausted tone."

I spent the 20 minute drive from Grand Rapids to Ofiara listening to Pearl Jam and having the music interrupted by what Jill had said. The conversation was nothing new, it was the same conversation we had, once a week, for four years. This time, however, it seemed different. There was a touch of consignment in her voice, a goal. She was going to do something, I could feel it. I knew she wouldn't do anything to intentionally hurt me, but she might do something to pull me out of my comfort zone.

Honestly, Jill could have done much better than me. She was smart, creative, and very pretty. Her face was framed by blonde hair which accented deep blue eyes. This was in contrast to my short brown hair and often dumpy disheveled look. Additionally, my intelligence was based more on practicality.

Driving through town in the late spring was like a dream. When I was little, Ofiara seemed isolated from the rest of the world, like some sort of Brigadoon the world had forgotten. Things were just turning green and the smell of grass clippings hung in the air. Most of the roads in Ofiara were still gravel, with only Main Street and a handful of other streets paved. There were multiple oak trees growing on either side of Main Street leading down to the lake, providing nearly complete shade cover for those headed for the solace of the water.

I decided to park at my house and walk the three blocks to the grocery store. The early morning silence was almost overwhelming as I opened the car door and stepped out to my gravel driveway. I started down the road to the store.

There was a breeze coming off the lake and green lilies were starting to push through the soil in a few flower beds in yards along the road. Through the trees I could see the reflection of the sun on the waves of Lake Ofiara.

There had been a stray sheep dog or some sort of mixed breed hanging around town for weeks. His color was off-white with streaks of brown and black on his head and tail. That particular morning he was wandering from yard to yard, peeing on everything in his path.

The giant hairy dog reached an area twenty feet in front of me directly in my path. He sat on the sidewalk ahead for a moment as if to acknowledge we were the only two souls on the street that early Sunday morning. He tilted his head and let out a soft bark, like he wanted me to stop and talk.

"Hi there," I said with a smile and laughed quietly, hoping no one had seen me talk to the town stray that morning. I walked past him and across the street towards the grocery store.

Jill's demands for a formal commitment again ran through my head. The more I thought about it the more anxiety I felt. I didn't want my world interrupted. I liked things the way they were.

Unlocking the store's front entry I looked down the road at the lake, wishing it was summer already. I wanted to be down at the beach feeling the water on my feet and grilling with friends. I just wanted to be anyplace but inside. Inside was closed in, dark, and always seemed so far from the fun.

The thing about Ofiara was that, aside from continuous economic struggles, most people would have agreed it was a great small town. It was filled with beautiful houses, very few fences, and tall oak trees. For the residents of Ofiara, it was a home, not simply a place. Ofiara, the place I had always called home, was a town of a little under five hundred people. The main industry was a manufacturing plant called In-House, which made ventilation materials. The plant was a subsidiary of a larger manufacturing corporation, which was a part of yet another larger conglomerate. In other words, In-House was owned by a faceless group who would never step foot in town.

The group of unknown In House investors had taken advantage of a financially desperate situation on Iron Ore Range in Northern Minnesota in the 1980s. Communities on the range were economically dependent on the mining industry, an industry which was falling quickly into a deep hole. When the venting plant moved into town the investors knew those individuals in Ofiara were desperate. In fact, they knew the residents of our small town would have been willing to accept jobs with almost any terms or demands they made. The management of the future ventilation plant knew low wages are still something, and something is better than nothing.

Then, in the early 1990s another change would come to Ofiara. Employees of In House became tired of their low wages. My dad was one of the tired plant employees. He was also the one to initiate the possibility of a union and the other workers started to push for it. Of course, like most social change, it would not come easy. There were points when he was both the most hated and the most beloved person in town.

The workers at the plant were tired of feeling like they were being taken advantage of. Most had wages close to half of what they had earned in the mines, and they knew In-House was making money hand over fist. Management opposed the change because they knew the changes would mean a more slender profit margin.

There were threats, pickets, and a few punches thrown. In the end the workers won. Wages increased by twenty five percent, putting many of the workers closer to the same wages they would have earned working in the mines. In addition to this, the union covered all medical benefits and provided a small retirement plan. Of course, the downside of the union was that the workers had to use part of their wages to pay the dues which allowed them their extra benefits. This was a small price to pay for additional security and no one really complained.

Though the victory may not have been akin to planting a flag on the moon, the perseverance and strength for which they fought was a source of pride. Unfortunately, their success lasted for only a few short years. In-House's investors would again have the upper hand.

In the year 2007, ten people were given early retirement; my dad was one of them. Those ten people comprised almost exactly one fifth of the workforce. Factory management had told the workers that tax issues and overhead were forcing them to make some tough decisions. Really, there was only one decision and that was whether or not they would keep the plant open. The reality of what they were saying was that the larger conglomerate which owned the factory was starting to farm out some of its work to other places in the world, mainly south of the border. This economic blackmail was used consistently at In-House as a leverage tool for keeping wages low. Management understood the people of Ofiara definitively knew the consequence of economic hardship and they did not want to go back.

Following my dad's retirement he was elected mayor of Ofiara. I would like to say that this was because he was an honorable man respected by all; unfortunately, it was because no one else wanted the job. Everyone in town knew he was the first person residents would turn to when the town struggled economically.

My dad was able to work with the plant and the workers for a few years, but there had been more whispers, rumors about possible lay-offs and the plant closing. Once again Ofiara was staring into the abyss and there were no prospects in sight. People were scared; especially those who had seen the town go through economic hardship in the past.

The store that morning was bustling with the Sunday shoppers gearing up for an afternoon of grilling and family. People rushed in and out of the store purchasing those early signs of summer such as ice-cream, burgers and chicken. By mid-afternoon the last of the buns and ground beef had been sold, and people had started to focus on hot dogs and brats. This resulted in at least six people complaining to me because they felt I did not order enough meat for such a nice weekend. Although I knew the individuals with the complaints were right, it didn't stop me from calling one man a "jerk" under my breath as he was leaving. It's always easier to have an opinion from outside of the situation.

When it finally started to quiet down I sighed with relief. I started restocking the shelves, my favorite part of a busy day. It made me feel as though I had accomplished something.

"Hey, your dad called, you better get over there now." My cousin Jason said smiling at me from behind the cash register. His face was covered with piercings and his black t-shirt gave him a rebellious look. Despite the outward appearance, Jason had a maturity which exceeded almost every adult I knew. He was overly responsible not only for himself, but also for everyone around him.

"You need help filling these shelves?" I asked putting my hand on an empty shelf behind me.

"No, it's OK, it won't take that long, and besides if you help me I will have nothing to do."

"Oh, no, I can help. He can wait a bit." I grinned walking over with a box of candy bars and placed them on the racks in front of the counter.

"Sarah, he is going to call again, and then he will nag, and then I will have to tell him you are just standing here." He looked at me for a reaction.

"Geez, OK." I said with a sigh.

"OK then!" He said with a grin.

"Hey, Jason, I noticed there is an open bag of dog food in the break room. Have you been feeding that stray sheep dog?" I asked.

Jason smiled "I'm not going to say anything self-incriminating. What I will say is that any food given to Monet was purchased from the store. So, it's none of your business."

"You didn't name him?" I asked with a disapproving look.

"It's ok; I think he liked the name."

"Ok," I said with a sigh putting the last of the candy bars neatly in place. "See you at my dad's after you close up?"

"Maybe, if you're lucky," Jason said.

I started walking to my parent's house. The streets were much busier than early that morning but it gave me a chance to stop and chat with people along the way. There weren't a lot of deep discussions but it was nice. The thing is, those conversations may not have many words, but there is a historical context. Their hopes, dreams, failures, and success are all weaved into the culture of such a small town. I already knew a fair amount about other members of the community. A short talk was simply an update on a story.

It wasn't until I had walked down the alley leading to my parent's yellow arts and crafts style home that I realized I still had my apron on. I took it off mid-step smelling fresh baked bread in the air. It was the smell of comfort.

As I walked into the house, I saw my mom standing over the stove in the kitchen, going through every single detail, always wanting things to be perfect, always wanting to make people happy. I couldn't help but smile at the image of her, in shorts, listening to some obscure jazz music I had never heard before. She was just so cool.

On the surface my mother seemed like the sort of person who was a traditionalist, but as with all people, things are never that simple many people have a tendency to habitually put others in a box in an attempt to identify and label them. This didn't work with Louise. At sixty four years old, she was one year my father's elder and could have passed as my older sister. She was tall and thin with her hair cut into a bob.

My mom was a musician. She decided to settle down with my dad rather than spend years on tour. Maybe she could have been famous, but we will never know. If she did have regrets they never surfaced. She spent a lifetime making herself and those around her happy. In my mind it took a smart and complicated person to think in the same way as my mother.

"Can you grab the forks Sarah?"

"Yes Mom."

My mom looked over and smiled at me. "I was thinking, next week maybe, we could go shopping in Minneapolis."

"Yeah?" I asked.

"We could get you some new clothes. Something to update you a little. Something to make you feel new."

My forehead wrinkled up a bit. "Hmmm, I'll think about it." I knew this was my mom's attempt to make me more presentable and a little less tomboyish. I usually wore a t-shirt and jeans, sometimes a dress shirt. It was her attempt to remake me so I would meet a guy, settle down, and give her grandchildren.

My mom smiled. "Seriously, you're not getting any younger; show it off while you have it."

I smiled back. "Nothing pink, flowered, or ruffled." I said as I grabbing a hot cheddar pierogi out of a bowl on the counter and popping it in my mouth.

"Of course not," she agreed, but I could see those wheels of hers turning.

I helped my mom for a while, avoiding talking to my dad. I made myself look busy because it was easier than talking to him. He was always either in the garage or camped out at the grill. He loved being the center of attention and winning the approval of those who would gather for his Sunday meal tradition. It was a day he would straighten out any family business. If something needed to be discussed or a project needed to be done it would be done on Sunday. That is the way it had always been as far back as I could remember.

I heard my dad's voice. "Sarah, come out here for a minute."

I walked outside to the front of the garage where my dad was standing by the grill. His salt and pepper hair complemented a red Hawaiian style shirt.

"Hey," I said.

"How are things going at the store?" he asked.

"Good, but I am not going to get rich anytime quick."

"Summer is coming and business will pick up a bit."

I smiled and sat down on a lawn chair close to my Dad. I wasn't sure what he was cooking but it smelled like barbecue sauce. My dad used a ton of sauce on almost everything he cooked. My theory was that he did this to offset the temperature he cooked at which was most often too high, charring the meat until it was close to inedible.

"Is everything else OK?"

"Yup," I said looking at the ground, wishing for a cigarette. Ironically, I didn't smoke but it seemed like it would be a good time killer during the awkward silence. It was the same lack of verbal exchange which appeared in almost every conversation I had alone with my dad. The hopeless gap in conversation that gave me a chance to look uncomfortably around and think for a moment about what Jill said.

For just one moment, it was on the tip of my tongue, the confession to my father, telling him I was a big old flaming lesbian. Fortunately, the urge to confess quickly passed. It was replaced by the image of my dad calling me something derogatory. Really, that was the outcome I envisioned, just pissing my dad off and bringing shame to the family.

Another way I would always validate my fear was by telling myself that coming out was my burden, not one my family should suffer. Why should they suffer the consequences? Why should I tell them to make myself feel better? The answer, at least the way in which I formulated it in my mind, was quite simply that my dad and I lived in two different worlds. His world was one of fairness, where hard work could get you anything, including the admiration and respect of others. My world was close to the same with one exception and that was no matter how hard I worked there would be a moral majority which would hate me or at the very least find my lifestyle vile and disgusting.

Finally, my dad boldly broke the silence. "I have been talking to Polar Beverage about the possibility of moving a bottling plant into town."

Polar Beverage was one of the top three manufactures of soda and bottled water around the United States and the rest of the world. In fact, I had a large display of Polar Beverage products at the entry of the store. Their main product was dark soda laden with corn syrup, called Venin. Of course, there was also Diet Venin, for those who were conscious about their figure. Another of their very well known products was the upscale bottled water called Voleur d'O. Tourists would often come into the store and purchase the transparent liquid for close to three dollars a bottle. I couldn't taste a difference between the expensive water and regular tap water. It just seemed unethical to sell something people could get for free, right out of the tap.

"Why are you trying to get a beverage company to move into Ofiara?" I asked.

"In-House Venting is talking about the possibility of another lay-off in the next few months. I think they are slowly trying to move the whole operation to Mexico or some other bullshit," my dad said as he continued to poke the meat on the grill.

I walked over to the cooler on the ground and pulled out a beer.

My dad continued "We have to be ready for them to pull out, because if they do, we will be screwed just like in the '80s."

A small laugh escaped my lips when I thought about how my dad had worded his sentence.

My dad looked at me with his eyebrows furrowed in irritation "Sarah, I don't think this is funny."

At that moment I saw Father John walking up the driveway. His muscular build and perfect hair always seemed to negate the possibility that he was a man of the cloth. John had been my best friend since the first day we met in kindergarten. It was very difficult for me to think of him as a priest. He was the person with whom I had shared my first beer and a great deal of pot.

"Father John," my dad said walking towards him and extending his right hand.

I cannot remember ever having shaken my dad's hand.

"Donald," said John grabbing my dad's hand and giving it a firm shake.

I knew that my dad secretly wanted me to marry John. John was one of those guys, whom you never questioned, because he was always honest; he wore his integrity on his shoulder. He was that friend who was always there for me and I knew how lucky I was.

My dad's next dinner guest was walking up the driveway, my brother Eric sporting a case of beer. He looked a little like me, only a few inches taller and hair cut short. Eric had worked for the venting company since a few months before his high school graduation. He hated In-House. It always seemed like he was looking for something different, something new. He would talk about moving to California or Mexico. Really, he just wanted to feel like he had choices. Just like everyone else, he wanted to know that if he had a dream, he would be able to follow it.

"Father, I was just on my way to confession," Eric said in his cool voice.

"I'm not sure I have enough time to take your confession; you better schedule an entire day for that." John said with a smug grin.

"How is it going?" asked John.

"Good," Eric said, putting his beer cans in the cooler one by one.

"How is that militia group coming?" My dad asked. I could see the meat had started to lose all its moisture.

John looked over at me with a bit of a puzzled look.

"Oh my God, Dad, not every group that gets together out in the country constitutes a gun toting militia."

"When did you start a militia?" asked John cracking a sarcastic grin.

"Father, keep up, not a militia." Eric replied looking over at my dad to make sure he was still turned away. He then looked at John pretending he was smoking a joint.

"Nice." John said getting a beer out of the cooler.

"Oh yeah," Eric said smiling.

"Militias are a part of American tradition as old as the United States. You have to be able to protect your family," my Dad said, looking at Eric.

"Again, and for the final time, it is not a militia," Eric stopped and looked at my dad, "that is your dream, not mine."

"That is not my fucking dream," my dad said getting a little defensive. "My dream is to have a happy, healthy family."

I found more than a few problems in my dad's assertion that Eric had started a militia or was involved in any sort of militant behavior. Eric was a diehard pacifist. When Eric and I were young, my dad used to take us hunting. Eric would almost never shoot, and when he did it was always a miss. On the other hand, I would shoot, but I got buck fever every time, shaking so hard I was afraid I would pass out, or worse, cry, in the middle of the woods.

"Dad," Eric said "we go out to the cabin and talk and hang out. That is it and nothing more. We don't have guns; no military style drills, and most of all we are not planning for Armageddon. Apocalyptic thinking is the product of people who either are either bored or have shitty lives."

My dad gave Eric a glare and turned back to the grill where he started removing the crispy meat from the grill.

Listening to them bicker was like listening to two separate conversations at once. Neither one was ever really hearing what the other had to say but they sure as hell wanted to make sure they were heard.

"Alright, I understand you have every right to go play with your friends. Anyway, dinner is ready."

Eric rolled his eyes as the four of us started to walk inside.

John pulled me back for a moment by the arm. "You need to tell your Dad."

I smiled "I am not ready yet. Are you channeling Jill this afternoon?"

"Well, she called, but that isn't the point. Living a lie is never a good thing Sarah," John said.

"Neither is my dad calling me a dyke or him having another heart attack," I smiled. "Let's go eat," I said, grabbing John's hand while pulling him inside.

I looked around the table as everyone dug in. With the exception of my mom everyone looked as if they were on a feeding frenzy after not eating for a week.

"Jacqueline came into the store this morning Mom; she said I should say hi to you," I said.

"What about me?" my dad asked.

"Jacqueline asked where you were this morning. She said she didn't see you at church."

Eric gave me a sour look. He and Jacqueline had a history.

My dad let out a short laugh. "I was meaning to go, headed in that direction. Does that count?"

"Really?" asked my mom.

"Oh yes." My dad responded not looking at my mom.

John grinned and looked directly at my dad. "It would be great to see you there, Donald."

"I would like to point out Sarah's attendance at church is non-existent." Eric said with a grin looking over at me and taking a drink of red wine.

I rubbed my ear, then flipped Eric the bird.

"In all honesty, Jacqueline's church attendance could use some improving as well." John said with a smile. "I think the mothers of priests just sort of assume a free ticket to the big H."

"Say Dad, have you heard any news about what is going on at the plant?" asked Eric taking a huge bite out of what we had discovered was chicken.

"Honestly, I'm not sure how concerned we need to be at this point; nonetheless, I'm trying to pull in another manufacturing plant."

"Why? Do we really need another business to fail?" asked Eric.

"Thank you, Mr. Positive." I said. Eric smiled and we both laughed.

"I just don't see the point, and I apologize for sounding negative. Towns all around us are losing money, people, and businesses. It seems like we are just spitting into the wind." Eric said.

"We have to at least try, don't we?" asked my mom in a stern but kind voice.

"Point well taken," said Eric.

"Why can't we do something like some sort of an employee owned business?" John asked.

"Because, we are not some sort of commies living in a socialist country." My dad responded without even looking up from his dinner.

"I am not sure that is socialist or communist." I said.

"What about Harley Davidson?" John asked.

"That is one example of a single business out of thousands of employee owned businesses which have failed." My dad replied. "That kind of business does not work. It creates too many cooks in the kitchen if you know what I mean."

Eric rolled his eyes, but I knew what my dad meant, and I have to say I agreed with it. If the few people who worked for me at the store were part owners the miniscule profit I made would be non-existent.

"If we get a new plant are you going to apply?" John asked Eric.

"Hell, yes," Eric smiled "All the pop I could drink, oh yeah."

My mom got a devilish grin on her face. "You know, Memorial Day weekend is coming soon."

"Yes Mom, we know that," Eric said, pouring another glass of wine.

Looking at me, my mom said, "That means a lot of single men."

"Oh geez," I muttered under my breath.

John gave me a look of disapproval.

After dinner I said my goodbyes and drove back to Grand Rapids. I just wanted to settle in for the night with Jill. I didn't like hiding her from my family, but I just did not feel I had the strength to tell them. Although my family was Catholic, they were not particularly homophobic with the exception of my dad.

My father constantly made jokes about the queer community. He would get angry when he heard anyone talking about gay marriage. His argument was that he did not feel same-sex couples should be allotted the same benefits as heterosexual couples because it would bring down corporations economically. The idea that homosexuality was going to bring down the corporate world was far beyond my realm of thinking. Maybe I just wasn't smart enough to understand this strange logic. It sounded like something he had heard from some conservative talk show. In all fairness to my dad, he was a product of his generation. Regardless of how he came to this conclusion, the way he voiced those thoughts didn't create an open venue for discussion. How could I open myself to the possibility of that sort of anger and animosity being directed at me?

I found myself chin-deep in the conundrum of a lie. No matter how intimidating and frightening the truth, the lie drives a wedge far more damaging. It creates an irritant which distracts from the rest of the relationship. The entire connection between two people ends up being artificial, build on a fake history. It becomes built on ideas of who the other person should be rather than who they actually are.

The first person I told about being a lesbian was John when we were in high school. He was the one person I knew could keep a secret. I was so afraid he would hate me or think I was sick. What actually happened was that John hugged me tight and for what felt like several hours while I sobbed. No matter how honest I had been with myself and him that day, in the end I felt flawed and broken. I was a realist. I knew that no matter how hard I tried in life, no matter what I was able to accomplish, there would always be someone who would hate me because of who I loved.

After high school, I attended the University of Minnesota in Minneapolis. It was far enough from home that my parents couldn't just show up unannounced every other weekend. However, it was close enough that I didn't have to spend half my student loan on travelling back and forth. I had spent years being dishonest about my sexuality with those around me. Being away from home gave me a chance to know myself better. I needed to come to terms with my insides.

In Minneapolis I was able to almost feel a sense of acceptance within a small group of friends, a group of people who understood. Ironically, I still had my personal homophobia to overcome. There was that piece of me that wanted to be normal, to fit in, to live the American dream. Why couldn't I fall in love with a man and have children? Why was it that I did not get the white picket fence?

After college I moved home to Ofiara and worked as an accountant for a firm in Grand Rapids. It didn't take me long to realize a life of accounting really wasn't the thing that was going to fill my life with happiness and bliss. It became clear I would have to look for something else.

A few years later my dad started to push me in the direction of becoming a business owner. The Main Street grocery store in Ofiara was up for sale. After months of my dad pushing me my will power was gone and I bought the store. My brother shook his head at my decision and couldn't understand why I would want to create a stronger bond with the town.

It was only two days after I bought the store that I met Jill at a club in Minneapolis. I instantly fell in love. She was talking with some friends of mine and in that immediate moment, before even talking to her, I wanted to be with her. We dated long distance for a few years and I found myself traveling to Minneapolis at least once a week. However, Jill being a passionate person, another year of long distance would have been too much. She was able to find a job as a mental health therapist in an outreach program in Grand Rapids. I was so excited when she moved closer because we were able to see each other more often. However, the move also meant the pressure was on. I would eventually also have to make a move.

Jill was very goal-oriented and had very specific ideas about how she wanted her life to be. What she wanted was a job, a partner, and possibly one day children. The difficult part was that sometimes I felt as though her goals did not leave room for mine.

When I arrived in Grand Rapids that evening Jill had the windows open in the house and was sitting on the sofa reading, her hair tucked behind her head.

I tiptoed up to the window and yelled, "Boo!" I giggled as she jumped.

"Hey dear, how was dinner?"

"Good. How's the book?"

"It's ok."

"Yeah?" I replied.

I walked inside and sat down next to her on the couch. I kissed her and said, "Please know Jill, I am very aware of the fact that I am lucky."

"You better know it," she laughed.

"Yes, yes I do," I smiled.

"Have you decided if you are telling your parents or not?" Jill asked.

"You know when you have to do something, the right thing, and you feel frozen."

She smiled "I think I do."

"I feel that way, and I am not sure how to get over it. I love you, but I am scared."

Chapter 2

Memorial Day weekend arrived with a 90 degree Friday. The heat was a sign the summer would be much warmer than usual. I could see the lake from the front window of the store. I wanted to be there, wading in the water or laying in the sun.

Making matters worse, the restaurant patio next door was packed with tourists. People were eating, talking, and laughing. One man was having a Bloody Mary for breakfast. It looked so damn good.

All that morning locals had been walking into the store talking about how there had been five more lay-offs at the ventilation plant. Moreover, management had threatened there would be more. My dad was trying desperately to figure out if these actions were some sort of a bluff in union negotiations.

Eric said the plant was getting fewer and fewer orders. He said that the missing orders were being sent to a plant someplace in Mexico. It was a place south of the border where the company could pay lower wages and not have to worry about negotiating with a union. It was corporate heaven where those pesky rules in the United States did not matter.

A nice change of pace came late in the morning when some friends showed up at the store.

"Good morning," Jake, a muscular well dressed man yelled with a smile.

"What are you up to today?" I asked.

"Jake and I are on a three day holiday from the paper mill!" Todd said in a laid back tone. In his flannel shirt and shorts he looked like he was headed to see the Grateful Dead.

Jake and Todd had both attained jobs at the mill when they were going to the community college in Grand Rapids. Both had majored in paper science and both planned to retire from the mill. Sometimes I thought both shared a brain.

"Off till Tuesday!" yelled Jake from several aisles away.

Jake was one of those guys who always wore dress shirts and pressed jeans and trying to be a ladies' man. Unfortunately for him, he usually came off as a pervert.

I didn't ask any more about their time off. Danny, the other person shopping with Jake and Todd had been laid off from one of the mines and had not been able to find work in months. She was looking down the barrel end of applying for an extension on her unemployment benefits. It was difficult for most people to find work and even more difficult for someone who had a criminal record. That was Danny's burden; she had done one thing for which society would not forgive her for seven years.

The three of them brought steak, potatoes, and lettuce to the counter.

"Party tonight?" I asked. "Grilling maybe?"

"No," said Jake with a grin. "We're meeting for a prayer group later."

"Oh," I said with a pause. I had this need to find out what the heck they were doing or at least be invited to eat. Even though I had no plans to go, it would have been nice to be invited.

"You coming over?" asked Jake.

"Oh, I think I am headed for Grand Rapids tonight." I said.

"Your loss, baby," said Jake. "I was going to give you a chance to make out with me later."

"Shut up," Todd said slapping him on the back of the head. "Why do you have to be such a pervert?"

"I have to try and make up for the gay factor," Jake said.

Todd squinted at Jake "What the hell are you talking about?"

Jake replied "We are always together. I don't want people thinking we are gay."

Danny sighed "You know, it doesn't matter what's in his head. Eventually, it all comes out. Like vomit." She looked at me and squinted though a pair of dark-rimmed glasses as though she was trying to see something. "You are always going to Grand Rapids, like it is somehow more interesting than our little metropolis."

The long pause and intense look she gave me said she had already made up her mind on what I was doing regardless of what I said. I could understand how Danny's attitude could intimidate some people. Everything about her seemed precise and harsh. Her short dark hair always covered part of her face as though she was trying to hide something.

Jason walked into the store, obviously fresh from the beach. His blonde hair looked a little greasy from sunscreen the smell of which filled the room. Following him back to the stockroom was the stray sheep dog who had been wandering around town had followed him and sat outside the front of the store.

"Hey, you're late, buddy." I said with an instigating grin.

"I think not, I am in fact ten minutes early; you're just jealous because you wanted to be down at the beach."

"Yep," I said as the phone rang.

I looked down at the caller ID, recognizing my Dad's number.

"Does he know my schedule?" I asked as Jason walked quickly to the counter and picked up the phone.

"Main Groceries," he said looking at me. "Yes, she is here; hold on Uncle Don."

I sighed and took the phone, "Hi Dad."

"Can you come over when you are done with work?" he asked.

"I was headed to Grand Rapids for a while; can it wait till later?"

"No, this is important."

I hung up the phone and whispered, "Damn it."

Walking to my Dad's, I reviewed the things he typically rated as important. It was the time of year he may have wanted me to help him put his boat into the water. There was also a chance he wanted to talk about my brother. He had some concerns about what Eric was going to do if In-House should close. It didn't matter; to my dad it was always important and imperative.

I was pondering what task my dad could have in mind. The day was so beautiful and warm it seemed sad to waste it on a dramatic or busy evening. I walked the long way, around the block to the front of my parent's house. When I turned the corner, I realized what he wanted to talk about. Jill's car was on the road in front of my parent's house.

"Damn it!" I said as my face flushed red. I stood out on the sidewalk for what felt like twenty minutes, looking away from the house at the street. I was scared and just wanted the moment to be over. Running was not an option, nor was denial. Either choice would have meant losing Jill and whatever integrity I had left. My face felt hot and my body was shaking. I searched the ground for some invisible magic button which would allow me to undo the moment. I needed something that would allow me to go back in time and avoid the phone call from my dad.

When I turned back to the house my dad was standing right behind me.

"Why did you think you could not tell me this?"

"I am so sorry, Dad," I started to cry.

"I wish you did not have to go through this." He held me tighter, "I will always be proud."

I looked up to see my mom. She paused, giving the majority of the moment to my dad, and then walked softly across the yard. Her graceful steps set me at ease. If she had been angry she would have been walking much more quickly.

My dad released his grasp, making room for my mom.

"Sarah, you have someone waiting out back." She hugged me and whispered, "I like her." She held my shoulders and looked me in the eyes. "You know what is scary, is thinking that your daughter will be alone for the rest of her life because you can't see her letting someone in."

When I walked in, I looked at Jill who immediately smiled. What she had done felt scary, difficult, and most of all, it felt right. It wasn't until that moment that I realized what she had done freed me.

The four of us sat and talked for a couple hours. My parents absolutely grilled Jill for information about herself, making sure their daughter was not dating a drug dealer or an unemployed serial killer. My mom was sad horrified Jill and I had been together for so many years and were not living together or made a formal commitment.

My dad left the room several times to go outside with the phone. My guess was he was contacting the soda company, trying to seal the deal.

Later, my brother stopped by. He didn't seem particularly shocked by the information, but hugged me and said he was happy. It was relatively clear that Eric probably knew but never said anything.

After the very emotionally draining afternoon, Jill and I drove over to my brother's to have a drink. If ever there was a time to have a drink, it was that evening. I still felt the anxiety and rush of having been forced out of the closet.

Eric lived about five miles out in the country, down a few different dirt roads, one of which did not even have a name. If a person didn't know the area, they would never be able to find his house. There were three cars in the driveway, but no lights on in the house.

"Where is everyone?" asked Jill.

I sighed "We are going to have to walk for a bit."

A mulched path led us to the back of the house and down a hill through a wooded area. There were dense trees on both sides of the path as the mulch merged with a dark grey soil.

"Is this where your brother buries the bodies?" asked Jill.

"I will tell you about this area later," I whispered.

We reached the edge of a heavily wooded lake. There was no wind creating a stillness which allowed a person to hear sounds from miles away. The full moon reflected off the placid water. In a clearing, just feet from the lake, stood a small cabin that looked as if it had been there for a hundred years.

There was a musky smell inside the structure which reflected its age. My brother and friends were drinking beer and playing on their laptops. The reason the four of them were out in the middle of the woods with their electronic toys was because my brother and Danny were not actually allowed to own computer equipment.

Just after Eric had turned 18, he and Danny had started hacking into computers as a hobby. The two had decided one day to pull a Robin Hood and hack into a bank. It wasn't just any bank; rather, the bank was known for making loans to developing countries under the thin disguise of progress. The loans offered by that particular bank were like a deal with the devil and came with a hefty price. Oftentimes this price would be something such as privatization of the countries' water or other utility systems. Privatization of something which had previously been municipal created a venue where a service, a product, or a good which would normally be something the government provided at an affordable price, became a luxury item. Something as basic as water became almost unattainable for the poor and even a large part of the middle class.

Eric and Danny took matters into their own hands because they felt if they did not do something, nobody would. They stole hundreds of thousands of dollars and routed the money towards an overseas fund which sought to build water wells in underdeveloped countries. No one other than Eric and Danny ever had any idea just how much. The money was never found. There wasn't enough evidence to give them prison time, so instead they each received seven years of probation.

The only reason Eric and Danny were caught was because they had used the school's computers to hack into the bank. One of the teachers from the school had figured out someone was using the school's system to rob banks. John's mother Jacqueline had been the teacher. That is when she became the focus of Eric's animosity. He felt she was adding to a structural evil and assisting repressive economic forces which would decimate several developing countries.

Sadly, Jacqueline did not know who had broken into the computer system. Quite simply, she knew someone had done something wrong. She felt she had no choice other than to alert the authorities, leading federal agents to our small town.

Eric and Danny both lost their scholarship money and any hopes of getting into a good college. Eric's summer job turned into his career, when college became out of reach. Danny's mother got her a job at one of the mines.

The very sad part was that Jacqueline was no stranger to human rights issues. She had taken many trips to different parts of the country and the world. She kept a picture on the wall of her classroom, of her being tear gassed at a protest against the Vietnam War. Jacqueline was just a strong believer in human rights as Eric and Danny; they just viewed solutions very different.

The cabin had a small kitchen, a bathroom, one bedroom, and a main living room. Eric and his friends were seated around a giant oak table which took up a third of the room. Jake was smoking, making the air heavy and thick.

"Hey Sarah, I hear you are gay now." said Jake with a smile.

"That's the rumor," I replied.

Jake grinned and raised his eyebrows.

"And, by the way, this is Jill."

"It was Jake wasn't it? Jake made you want to go to women." Todd said seriously. "I hear he does that a lot."

"Shut up, ass face," Jake replied.

"You know, this gives me a good reason to hit on you even more." Jake said.

"Hey Jill, I'm Danny," Danny said, giving a small wave.

Jake stood up for a moment to shake Jill's hand. "I am Jake and very pleased to meet my competition."

"Likewise," Jill said with a mischievous smile.

Just then the door opened and John walked in.

"Good evening, Padre" said Danny.

"Hey there!" John said. "So, this is the militia group? It's not quite how your dad described it."

"Not a militia group, John" Eric said with a sarcastic tone.

"So what is it?" John asked.

"Who the hell knows?" Todd laughed.

"Who cares, is the more important question." Jake replied in response to Todd.

"What is John up to tonight?" Eric asked.

"I am doing the 'Jesus likes to hang out with the sinners' thing. You know he always liked to go where the action was."

"Sweet!" exclaimed Jake.

"They are attempting to get prison time," I said.

"Hey, good job," John said.

"Actually, what the more constructive individuals among us are doing is collecting data on companies which have economically benefited from war," said Danny without even looking up.

"Sounds like a big job," Jill said.

Danny sighed and smiled.

I mixed three vodka gimlets, giving one to John who had seated himself on a bar stool next to the door. Jill and I sat down on a love seat on the opposite end of the room.

John looked over at me, fishing ice out of his drink "Your dad called me today. He wanted to let me know you're a lesbian. He said that because I am your friend I should know."

A surge of concern ran through my body. "Did he seem OK with it?"

"He seemed OK."

There was a hard knock on the cabin door and a women's voice outside yelled. "Eric, if you have computer equipment, hide it and open the door! I don't want to see what you are doing, but I have to come in!"

The four computer nerds rushed to hide both the computers and a small bag of pot which had been sitting on the middle of the giant table.

"OK, we are decent!" yelled Eric.

Terry, an Akin County deputy walked in. She graduated the same year, from the same school, as John and I. She was homecoming queen, head cheerleader, and was most likely the most high maintenance law enforcement officer in the state of Minnesota. Yes, she was beautiful, but in that sort of orange fake tan, plastic way. She was also John's high school sweetheart. After dating for years, Terry broke it off around graduation. The breakup pretty much devastated John, which was why he no longer liked her. However, we lived in a small town. People living in close proximity to one another and we really did not have a choice other than to get along. It's funny though; whenever she showed up someplace that John was, I got the sneaking suspicion she was fishing, seeing if he still held a candle for her.

"How you all doing tonight?" she asked.

"Good, we were just praying with the Father." said Todd.

"Yeah, OK." She paused and looked down. "Sarah, your dad said you would be here. There was an incident in town tonight and I was wondering if you guys had heard anything."

"What happened?" asked John as he continued to play with his drink, trying to fish out a filbert nut from beneath the ice. It was a thin veil which helped him avoid eye contact with Terry.

"A Mexican farm worker who came into town to get some groceries was jumped outside your store." Terry said looking at me.

"Is he ok?" I asked.

"His face is pretty banged up."

"Who did it?" asked John in a tone which illustrated this was something he took a bit personally.

"There were two guys and the worker did not see their faces. They told him they did not want to see him or any other Mexicans in town, taking jobs from Americans."

"Assholes," said Eric. "Sorry Father."

"That's ok, I am going to agree with that one," said John.

"Have you guys seen or heard anything?" asked Terry.

John kept on looking down and away. It seemed like Terry was John's reminder that at one time he had not been a priest and that of course he was a human. He was a man with feelings. Perhaps Terry was God's way of keeping John's humility high.

I gave out a soft sigh. "There are guys all over town who talk like that. The ones who think the In-House jobs are being shipped to Mexico. But, I don't know of anyone who would actually act on something like that."

Terry sighed. "I have federal agents coming in this month, because there are reports of a meth lab; the factory is facing more lay-offs, and now this."

"If we hear anything, we will let you know," John replied, without looking at Terry.

Once everyone knew Terry was well away from the cabin, the computers came out again.

"Well, there is one thing Terry rarely does," said Eric with a smile. "Her job."

"Hey," said John with furrowed eyebrows, in defense of Terry.

Eric in turn raised his eyebrows and said, "You know it's true John."

"Ok, yeah, you're right," John responded with a smile.

"Does anyone else see this as extraordinarily strange?" asked Todd looking around.

"What do you mean?" asked Jill.

"Racism in redneck alley? Yeah, not real bizarre." Jake responded loudly.

"Agreed, but physical violence?" asked Danny.

"So, are hate crimes normal in town?" asked Jill.

"Nope," I replied. "This is a small town and if you do or say something derogatory to another person, it follows you and does not go away until you resolve it. If someone committed a hate crime, if they were that angry, someone would have heard about it."

My mother had always told me that violence was never as simple as one person hitting another; rather, words and actions can also be violent. A person could believe inside that they had never acted in a racist way, so their natural assumption would be that they were not a racist. However, that same person may silently think derogatory labels in their head or go out of their way to avoid the Mexican workers when they came into town. The same person who believes they are not racist can be the person who supports government policies which would typically have a negative effect on minorities.

Chapter 3

Two days later, on Memorial Day, my mom stopped at my house to pick me up. The two of us walked to Main Street, where people had started to gather waiting for the parade to start. Although there was a cool breeze coming off the lake, there was not a cloud in the sky and the sun was warm. When we got to Main Street, Eric was there waiting.

Groups of men and a few women, from every branch of the military, started to make their way down the street. There were multiple United States flags held very proudly by those who had walked through hell. My dad was one of those veterans.

It always caused a pain in my gut and made me think back to the stories my dad told about Vietnam, as well as the stories I knew he would never tell. He didn't choose to go to war; instead, he was drafted into Army. He told Eric and me about sitting in the rain for days, fires, bombs, and being so scared, his heart could have burst through his chest. Moreover, he told us about the terror that comes with armed conflict. The idea of knowing there are people with guns, pointed, ready to kill another human being. It was aiming a gun at another person or having one aimed at him.

My mind wandered across the ocean, to the next generation of soldiers who might one day be marching in the parade. The soldiers who were not with their families, who maybe had a gun pointed at them. The men and women who were in a desert so far away, in a war that was as hard to understand as violence itself.

Chapter 4

The summer weather continued to be beautiful, though that year was a bit dry and everything smelled like dust. Like every year, water became the main form of solace in Ofiara. Everyone in town under the age of eighteen spent most summer days at the lake. Those who didn't have enough ambition to walk the few short blocks to the lake were using kiddies pools or sprinklers.

Although the weather was nice, it was overshadowed by the increasing unemployment rate. Several more workers had been laid off from the plant. The disintegrating industry in Ofiara had started to feel like a band-aid being slowly pulled off. Our little world felt fragile, like a thin led crystal wine glass. The only businesses which continued to do well were the scattered resorts along the lake which were booked solid with tourists into the fall.

People were getting worried. One family, like a small group of refugees, left in the middle of the night leaving their home behind to be reclaimed by the bank. Although this tragedy had only happened to one family, their sudden absence shook everyone. It reminded everyone of their own vulnerability.

Making matters worse, there were rumors going around that a small group of high school students had been experimenting with, and perhaps selling, meth. Of course, teenagers' playing with drugs was not any big revelation in the 21st century. What was strange was no one was being able to identify either the source of the drug production or the names of any of those involved. Even cases of pain medication abuse in a small town were quickly identified, labeled, and discussed.

The more and more people talked about the meth, the more of a reality it became. This was regardless of the fact that nobody in town had yet identified who had been selling it. The overall perception was that the drug was brought to Ofiara from the city by outsiders. Big city hooligans were maliciously entering our small town with the intention of destroying our paradise. It wasn't odd or even paranoid thinking, considering that it was not the first time outsiders had taken advantage town folk.

Federal and state-level law enforcement arrived in town around the middle of June to investigate the claims of methamphetamine madness. People in suits and uniforms talked with townsfolk and searched though the area for some sign of either production or sales of the narcotic. Although most residents considered their presence intrusive and rude, they felt it to be a necessary evil. After all, they were the professionals; they would know better than the locals if there was a drug problem in Ofiara.

In the middle of the McCarthy-style investigation was Terry. She drove officers around, introduced them, and gave a synopsis of the meth issues which plagued our hometown. It looked as though the whole ordeal made her feel very important. It looked as though she was solving a crime.

After several days of detailed scrutiny nothing was found, not even a gram of the off-white, rock-like substance. Finally, the myth of the meth epidemic would be deemed a hoax and the outsiders left as quickly as they came. What they left behind was a sliver of doubt and paranoia. Neighbors would not be quite as trusting as they once were.

Chapter 5

City Council meetings were held in the Ofiara Community Center across the street from my store. It was a large colonial-style building with four white pillars in front. The building was the same venue which housed weddings, dances, and of course the occasional polka concert. The inside walls, which supported the twenty-foot high ceiling in the main hall, were painted a strange shade of light lime green. The strong musky smell permeating every room in the building was a by-product of several years of parties with all sorts of food and alcohol being spilled onto the hardwood floor. It was the center of all the town's activities.

Normally, the few people who showed up for the monthly meeting would be my dad, three to four members of the city council, and a handful of residents with requests and complaints. One person might ask permission to build an addition onto their house, while another may be there to discuss an intersection which needed a stop sign. Overall, it was by far one of the quieter events which would take place at the Center. The meeting that June, however, was slightly different.

I'm not sure why, but I loved watching my dad during meetings. He looked professional with his tie and a white dress shirt. He did well seeking solutions to problems. Unfortunately, that did not mean he was diplomatic. It always seemed like he was attempting to make all parties happy with a particular solution. Sometimes, that solution would be positive for everyone; however, more often than not, the solution could only be found in the lesser of two evils.

There were two people I did not recognize at the meeting. They had arrived early and sat at the front of the room, facing my dad and the rest of the council members. It was obvious the two men tried to dress down and blend in with the rest of the community. One of the men who looked like he was about fifty-five was wearing a Harley Davidson shirt. The other, a younger man about my age, was sporting a short sleeved plaid shirt. Both were wearing jeans and shoes far too expensive for the likes of Ofiara residents.

When the meeting was called to order new business was reviewed. There was one person wanted approval to build a garage. The request sparked a whisper from Eric, who wondered how anyone would dare to build something new with the local economy like it was. I gave Eric a look and shake of the head to let him know it was really none of his damn business.

The next person was an elderly woman named Ester, who her long grey hair pinned back almost comically in a bun. She was a cantankerous woman whose cheery side did not exist. She had a complaint about the number of stray dogs running loose in town.

"They're everywhere." Ester stated in an exhausted tone.

"Like where?" my dad responded.

"They wander the town at night. They dig up my flower bed," Ester said, handing my dad pictures of what I assumed to be her flower bed.

"Ester, this is more of a law enforcement issue." My dad said almost sugar coating the words. I don't think he did it to be nice. I think he was acting nice because he felt it would get her to sit down sooner.

Ester continued without missing a beat. "But they dug up my flowers."

"Again, there is nothing I can do."

Ester persisted "There must be something that can be done."

"Call Terry," My dad said, his patience visibly wearing thin.

With that, Ester walked to her seat. Like most participants, when she received her answer, she left quickly with little or no interest in anything else that would occur at the meeting. Honestly, there was a time I had felt the same way. Before my dad became mayor, I had never attended a city council meeting; did not really see the point. After attending the meetings for a few months, however, I became concerned. It always seemed there was something, some ingredient missing within the decision-making process. What was missing was input from those who were likely to be affected by the decisions made in that small building on Main Street.

Then it was Jacqueline Collin's turn. I could sense my brother's irritation as she walked to the front of the room.

Jacqueline walked slowly to the podium in front of the council members. She was in her sixties and wore her hair in a short bob. As she stepped up to the podium, I could see that she had a very serious look on her face. Unlike everyone else who had gone before her, she carried no papers or materials. Alexander, the secretary, asked for her name and address for the record.

"You know where I live Alex."

Jacqueline paused then cleared her throat. "Is there anything that can be done about the hate crime?" She looked directly at my dad as she spoke.

My dad spoke up, "Although I empathize with you Mrs. Collin, I am not sure what we can do about this. First we don't have any actual proof that there is something going on that could be specifically labeled as a "hate crime." Second, if we did have proof, what we need to do, as a community, is work with law-enforcement. If we work together as a community we can get things done."

I whispered to Eric, "I think she is right to be concerned."

"Yeah," Eric whispered back. "But she still irritates the piss out of me."

"First of all, an immigrant getting beat up because people are afraid he is going to take their jobs is in fact a hate crime. Secondly, isn't it your job to make sure we have a good and safe community?" asked Jacqueline.

"A community is everyone's responsibility." replied my dad. "I am not immune to responsibility any more than you are." My dad paused and continued "If you would like to do something I bet we can find a room here at the hall where you can hold meetings which would specifically address this issue."

"That is an idea. I will think about it and let you know," Jacqueline responded and walked from the podium to her chair directly behind me.

"We have one more piece of new business today." said my dad. "With us today we have two representatives from Polar Beverage Company. Polar is seeking approval to build a beverage bottling plant. The plant would sit on 5th Street and 10th Avenue West."

Both men stood up at the same time and walked to the podium together. One of the men was Douglas Kirkland, a young middle management guy from Minneapolis. The other, the one wearing the motorcycle t-shirt, was Peter Stafford, an upper management representative from Chicago. Despite their efforts to blend in, Peter was clearly unable to hide his metro sexual appearance.

Peter started to speak "We have a deal in place to buy the land at $400,000 and to start building the plant next month. We anticipate that within the first year, the plant will bring 50 jobs to the area."

My dad responded "Normally, the taxes on a piece of land that size would be relatively high, but the plant will not be directly on the lake. The city is also willing to grant you forgiveness on property taxes for the first year, a policy to be re-examined after that point."

I could hear Jacqueline mutter under her breath behind me, "This is stupid."

Peter seemed to have heard this also, as he paused slightly as he was talking.

Peter continued "Ok, so how about in return for this tax break, we will make a $50,000 donation to area schools the first year?"

With that statement almost everyone in the room was sold, except for Jacqueline.

"Silver tongued devil," I heard her whisper from behind me.

"Oh for fuck sake, Jacqueline," Eric said loudly. Although he had not meant to be heard, everyone did hear him, causing a short glare from our father. "Sorry," he said in a loud whisper.

"I think we have a deal," said my dad. "All in favor of the proposition signify your agreement by saying 'yes.'" My father and the council members all stated yes. "All those opposed please signify your disagreement by saying 'no.'"

Just as he said this Jacqueline raised her hand and said, "No."

"With all respect intended Mrs. Collin, this is a city council decision. We are going to do this with or without your approval," my dad responded without so much as a flinch.

"This town will benefit from this plant only on the week of the four Thursdays." Jacqueline said. I didn't understand what the four Thursdays meant; my assumption was that this was some sort of French saying which did not translate well. Jacqueline had not moved to the United States from Quebec until she was in her 30's. Although her English was good, it was sometimes confusing.

My brother let out a soft grunt under his breath. Eric may not have looked forward to having yet another manufacturing plant in town, but he was not going to agree with anything coming out of Jacqueline's mouth.

"I would like it to be on public record I oppose this decision. I would also like it noted that the entire town will regret this decision. This is a short-term solution that will not provide long-term benefits." Jacqueline stated.

"Your opinion is noted, Mrs. Collin." Alex stated careful to write down her words.

I may not have agreed with what Jacqueline said, but there was something unsettling about her words. It was in the conviction with which she said it. There was also that part of my soul that didn't trust a situation which seemed too good to be true. The problem was that it just didn't make any sense for her to oppose something which would offer so many benefits to her family, friends, and neighbors. The most pervasive question in my mind was why Jacqueline would make such comments as she did at the meeting. Unlike Ester, Jacqueline was not a bitter person who would come to a city council meeting and complain about the colour of the paint on park benches or an imagined epidemic of stray dogs. No, Jacqueline Collin was a well-respected part of the community.

Jacqueline had moved to the United States to teach French, but eventually went back to school and got a science degree. She spent many years working in the south and knew the consequences of poverty. It was same poverty which was sitting on Ofiara's doorstep. Jacqueline ended up in our town somewhere in the late 70's, where she stayed until she retired in 1999.

Towards the end of the meeting, I realized Terry was standing at the back of the room. When the meeting wrapped up, she walked to the front of the room and talked with Peter for a moment. This struck me as strange. It seemed odd to me that she even knew Peter. I thought perhaps she was casing out her next sugar daddy.

When I got home from the meeting, Jill was making cookies. She had given up her house in Grand Rapids to engage in domestic small town coupling with me. We were both unsure as to whether or not this was going to be a good decision. Our expectation was that we would face some sort of backlash, but we did not know what it would be.

"Hey, how was the meeting?" Jill asked.

After several minutes of telling her in detail about the meeting, she responded by telling me she really wanted to meet Jacqueline.

"You know, there is something good that may come from all of this," I said to Jill. "The store may make more money, and people might actually pay off their tabs."

There were thousands of dollars in unpaid accounts at the store which was on the verge of creating a substantial financial strain on me. It was difficult for me to turn people down, people I knew almost as family. People were coming in left and right asking for credit at the store, and most of the time I gave it to them. A loss of a few hundred dollars here and there was difficult, but not as difficult as seeing families I grew up with go hungry.

"Yes, that would be well and fine. But, what if Jacqueline is right?"

Although I agreed with Jill her question irritated me. I wanted to think about Polar Beverage as hope for the town. "For now, let's just hope she is wrong."

Chapter 6

It was July in Ofiara, which meant Water Carnival month. It was the time of year when Ofiara became the destination for thousands of partiers and vacationers. People from all over the state, and sometimes the country, would make the pilgrimage to take part in our town's festivities. Art and food vendors filled the park and the streets, making it impossible to drive a car through the downtown area. There were contests and activities, for which many individuals with the competitive spirit would spend the months before July planning. People would race beds against one another, up and down the main drag. There was one contest where teams were charged with building boats out of milk containers and race them over the lake. My personal favorite was the water fights. There was a ball looped to a rope and two teams would use fire hoses at full power, to push the ball past the other team's line on the rope.

My cousin Jason was lucky enough to have an art exhibit with his paintings and some sculptures, right next to the lake. Our family was very proud. The works he chose were brightly colored, almost surreal landscapes. There was almost always water present in his paintings and sculptures, illustrating the influence of growing up in a community built on the lake.

That year the celebration was slightly different, as the smell of the lake and food vendors was overpowered by the smell of new construction and diesel oil. The builders had started working on the Polar Beverage building on the first day of July. Echoes of trucks and large machinery could be heard throughout town. The chaos made people excited, because it offered hope.

The ventilation plant was down to a mere five workers. Additionally, those few workers were very tight-lipped and did not discuss the plant openly. However, what was ensued from their silence was the impending closure of In-House. Several town residents were very worried, but people were divided on who should take the blame. Some individuals felt the owners of the company were nothing short of traitors to America, because they were shipping work out of the country. Others blamed my dad, stating the town should have tried harder to keep the plant or initiated some sort of a tax break. There were others who would proclaim the housing boom was slowly dying down and In-House was simply being proactive, predicting a market which was doomed to decline.

A few individuals who had been laid off from In-House had been able to find work with the construction company charged with creating the new Polar Beverage building. Although the few jobs were welcome, it was not quite to the point of a solution.

There had also been two more hate crimes. One incident involving the painting of "the kkk is coming to get you race traitor" on the side of a farmer's truck. The vandals had not bothered to capitalize the initials for their organization. I assumed they hated education as well. The other incident occurred at the high school. One of the teachers, who happened to be black, left school late one evening and found a profoundly cruel note on his car. Using violent language, the note told the teacher he needed to leave town because he was not welcome. Fortunately, within a few hours of the incident, several people went to the teacher's home and let him know, they did not agree with the author of the note.

It was strange that the three acts had occurred within such a short period of time. There were a few people who felt the hate crimes were not mere acts of racism, but that, instead, the violence was a reflection of what was happening economically. People were looking for someone to blame. In-House disappearing and obscene amounts of individual debt had to be pinned to an individual or group. The problem was, if people could not find a person to blame, it meant the people pointing fingers would have to take a look at themselves and figure out how they had contributed to the problem. It was so much easier to blame others.

Adding insult to the economic injury in Ofiara was the foreclosure list in the Grand Rapids newspaper, which had grown from one page to four. For those who had their names appear on this list it was nothing less than complete humiliation. The banks could not have done anything worse had they paraded the families around town naked. Many residents were gossiping about who was going leave town. There would be no help, no fundraisers for these families; their financial weakness removed them from society.

Jacqueline came into the store the second morning of the carnival. She purchased enough food to feed five people for a week. Although she lived alone, this wasn't something all that unusual. When she came in, her purchases were mainly the few organic items I stocked in the store and never included animal products. A strict vegetarian, she didn't eat meat or eggs and always purchased a ton of produce. On some very rare occasions she would buy fish, if she had company. One time I asked her why she did not eat meat. She said it was the same reason she never got married. It was something to the effect of one being not ever being able to "own" another being.

Jason was helping me stock shelves before he went over to his exhibit. I had actually told him not to do this, but sometimes, it was like he just did not hear me. He would just go ahead and do what he felt needed to be done.

Monet watched Jason from outside, like a nine year old waiting for his best friend to finish his chores. I kept looking over at the dog and smiling. Finally, I walked over and opened the door to let him inside. He looked up at me as he walked in as though he was waiting for permission.

"Come on," I said, watching him walk to the side of the door and very politely sit down.

When Jacqueline pushed her cart next to the counter to pay I could see her eyes were red and glassy. Someone who did not know her may have thought she had been crying. People who did know her knew different.

"Are you having people over Jacqueline?" Jason asked. He knew the answer to the question and was just being polite, but I got a little irritated he had even asked it. It just seemed rude.

"No, I am using my glaucoma medication. I get hungry when I use it," Jackie replied without hesitation.

"Oh," said Jason. "Is it good?"

With that comment I gave Jason one of those looks which I had hoped would make him stop talking, perhaps for the rest of the day.

"Yes, I got it in Grand Rapids from a friend. Would you like some?"

"Sure," Jason said.

"Oh my God," I said in a whisper.

"Oh come on, Sarah," Jacqueline said. "This certainly does not seem like the worst crime in town. I highly doubt that police officer woman would give a shit unless someone paid her to care."

When she made that last statement about Terry, I had to work to hide my smile.

"I will try and stop in tonight, Jacqueline," said Jason.

A look of concern washed over my face, a look that Jacqueline noticed.

"Sarah, I called my liar, he told me the police were not going to arrest a retired teacher for pot. Besides, I have a prescription, it is for my eyes."

"Liar," I paused looking at her "You mean your lawyer? Your attorney?"

Jacqueline sighed, "Yes, that is what I said Sarah, my liar. You should come also, Sarah."

"OK," I said with absolutely no intention of going.

Jacqueline responded, "You need to lighten up a little."

"OK, I will keep that in mind," I said.

Jacqueline looked straight at me and said, "I heard you are living with a woman now." She got closer to my face and whispered, "A lesbian." She smiled and I went silent.

I felt myself go flush with my insecurities and fear. It made me feel a touch of that same anxiety I felt standing in front of my house only a month prior. I had hoped that not answering would make the kind interrogation of my best friend's mother just go away.

"You know Sarah, in other parts of the world this would really be no big deal. Not even enough to turn someone's head." She smiled such a beautiful and genuine smile, making me glad the moment had not gone away.

Jacqueline changed the subject exhibiting an attention span influenced by self-medication. "Jason, have you applied to colleges for next year?"

"Yes, I applied to the U of M and Minnesota College of Art and Design. My first choice is art school, but the University of Minnesota would not be bad either."

"You are very talented Jason," said Jacqueline, her face scrunching a bit. "You should be going off to New York or Paris. You need to fly away, little bird."

Jason smiled. "Thank you Jacqueline, that means a lot."

Jacqueline was right in saying he would do better in an environment which would allow him to grow. Jason, like me, was a little too attached to his home and Ofiara. Part of this was because he was the only child to a single mother, a nurse who worked too much and more or less lived for Jason. Jason was deathly afraid something would happen to him and she would end up alone.

Douglas, the Polar Beverage rep came into the store shortly after Jacqueline left. He asked if the company could set up an information booth to distribute free samples outside of the store, and I quickly approved. He unloaded the back of his truck in the alley behind the store, and carried case after case of products through the store. When he got everything out front he created a mountain of products produced by Polar Beverage Company.

The free soda was an obvious publicity stunt. It was thinly veiled as an act of generosity, an attempt to win over the people of the small town. Although it bothered me a little, I said nothing. My assumption was that the people of Ofiara were much smarter than that and would not be so easily fooled.

Douglas sat outside the store for the entire day handing out case after case of soda and water. He shook hands and made small talk with everyone who came through. It actually seemed as though he was running for mayor. In the end, everyone loved him; they could identify with him and his story. He told everyone how he grew up in a small town not that much different Ofiara and how he understood the issues and concerns of those living in this type of area. He also gave away every last can of soda and bottle of water.

After work that day, I walked over to the beach. The air smelled of tanning lotion and charred meat. Making my way through the crowded sand, I silently wished I could close down the store for the weekend and just enjoy being with family and friends.

Eric, Danny, and Jill were talking and grilling just a few feet from where Jason was set up. I was relatively sure this was Eric's idea, as he did not want Jason to have to miss out on any of the fun, because he had to be at a stand all day. Eric had always thought of himself as an older brother to Jason.

When I reached the table, everyone went quiet for a second as they looked over at me. They started talking again about the grill and whether or not they had brought enough beer.

"Hello dear," said Jill with a smile.

"Hey there," I said trying to sound slick, but instead sounding like the nerdy. "Yeah, I'm not sure that was what you were really talking about?"

"We were discussing Polar Beverage," said Eric.

"Some stuff," said Danny.

"So?" I asked, holding back a sigh of irritation.

"Apparently," Jill said with an indignant tone, "Polar Beverage has done some very bad things. Last year in a Colombian bottling plant, there was a dispute between the union workers and the company. The building that housed the union was set on fire and all three union leaders from that area were shot dead the next day. Everyone quit the union except two women, who refused. Two weeks later the women were pulled out into the street and shot in front of the whole town, including their small children."

I looked on pessimistically. "Ok, this has not been my experience with Polar Beverage so far. They seem nice. I am not sure I picture Douglas pulling people into the street and shooting them. Of course, I have been known to be wrong."

"The same basic events have been repeated in several countries around the world." Jill responded.

"It actually gets worse." said Danny.

There was a part of me that was getting very irritated. I was irritated at what they were saying. I was irritated at the possibility that it could be true. Most of all, I was irritated that Danny was spending so much of her free time looking into Polar, instead of looking for a job.

"What happened in India was just as bad, if not worse," Jill said.

"Polar Beverage built a water plant in India near a remote village." Danny took a drink of beer, and then continued to speak. "Within a year, the water supply for the entire village had dried up. They got funds from Universal Bank to build another well. Six months later, the second well had all but dried up. What was left was water polluted to the point it was undrinkable. And, there was too little to be used for crops."

"Then," said Eric loudly, "they had the audacity to sell water back to the villagers for more than the cost of a gallon of milk.

Jill then continued Eric's point, "Those same farmers could lose their farms. No water equals no crops, and no crops means no money. There will be no money to pay off the banks."

"Have you told Dad about this?" I asked Eric.

"Yes, this morning." Eric said, "But he said that we should wait and see what happens."

"Really?" I asked, even though I knew it was true.

"Yes," Eric answered

"Ok, I have to ask, and this is not because I don't believe you all but because I think someone should ask the question. Where did you get your information?"

"From the internet." replied Eric.

"I am not certain the internet is a reliable source." I replied skeptically.

"We used reputable sources," Eric stated with a hint of irritation. "All the information was attained through major newspapers."

"Is this the same internet that supplies pictures of the Loch Ness Monster, Yetis wearing swimsuits, and any type of pornography a person could ever want?" Everyone looked at me waiting for me to continue. "You know what? My issue with the internet is just this. People seek out the information they want to seek out, rather than looking at all sides and perspectives involved," I said a little more condescendingly than I should have.

"You know what? I am going to stop telling you things," Eric said.

"Don't I wish," I responded under my breath.

"Excuse me?" Eric returned with a sour look.

"Here's the thing. Dad is not always right about everything, but I think that we need to trust him. There have been no red flags so far. I think that if we run Polar off, we, and the entire town, have a lot to lose."

"Yeah, but don't you think that the town, the people who are going to economically benefit from jumping into bed with the devil should be able to make an informed decision? The direction the town is going should be up to more than just your dad and a few council members," Danny responded, fighting to make me hear their side.

"What if we tell the whole town and Polar hears that people are uneasy? What if Polar suddenly pulls out of the deal? Cuts their losses?" I asked. "If that happens, the town is then left without a choice anyway."

"So, the greater good is to keep our mouth shut and support this?" Danny asked. "I don't think so, it just seems wrong."

"If you were able to just pull this information off the internet, doesn't that mean its public?" I asked. "I would argue the town already has access to the information."

Eric replied, "Yes, most of the information came from major newspapers, but they were stories which only made the second or third page of the news. There is not a great deal out there which directly connects some of the violence to Polar Beverage."

"Isn't it plausible that some of this could merely be the rants of angry workers who were upset because they didn't get a raise?" I asked. "Could Polar's competition have planted the story?"

"Come on, Sarah," said Jill, getting a little short with me.

"Hey, it is a large, extremely huge corporation; would it not be unusual if things like this didn't happen?" I looked over at Jill. "I agree these things are horrible, but I am not sure that we can just jump to assumptions from the outside. I really don't think Polar Beverage is the Anti-Christ."

"If they are responsible for these tragedies, it's clear they have done nothing to be accountable for the damage they have caused." said Danny.

"I guess you have to do what you have to do; I just don't feel like playing a political poker game at the expense of the town," I said, a little irritated. I got a beer out of the cooler and sat down.

Jill looked at Eric. "Are you going to apologize to Jacqueline?"

"I already did," he said. "Danny and I both did."

Danny kept looking at me with this intense look, as though she was going to make me say what she wanted me to say, just by staring at me. I agreed that what they had told me was bad, evil, and morally reprehensible. What the company had done, if the allegations were true, made me sick. However (there is always that evil 'however'), these issues were not right in my backyard. Instead, what was in my backyard was the prospect of complete economic collapse for the entire town. My history, my family's history, my friends were all I could think about.

Jason walked over from his art stand, trailed by his furry companion. He took a drink of my beer. I gave him a disproving look and he just smiled.

"I know I came in late to the discussion here, but I have to say that Jacqueline is usually right on the mark when she says something. She really thinks Polar Beverage will be bad for the town," Jason said, grabbing a piece of cheese and offering it up to Monet.

"I hate to be the one to point this out, but we have other issues in town," I said, looking around, waiting for the attack. "In the last few months we have seen some profoundly awful acts of racism, people continue to lose their homes, and there is all this talk about meth dealers, maybe."

"I agree," Jason said, taking an uncooked hotdog and giving it to Monet.

"Ok, can we talk about something else, at least for the rest of the evening? Let's just enjoy the night," I said with a sigh.

"By the way, have you been home yet?" Jill asked me.

"No." I looked at Jill and asked, "Everything OK?"

"We have a new neighbor. Douglas Kirkland." Jill said, not sounding very gleeful.

"The Polar guy?" I asked.

Douglas had apparently decided to buy the house next door to mine. The house had been on the market for a few years. In the time since it had been placed on the market, I had claimed the lake shore in the back yard as my fishing area. His presence at the house put the kibosh on my fishing.

That night, in bed, Jill's irritation with me kept us both awake. I didn't agree with her on the urgent nature of the Polar Beverage issue, which she felt had to be addressed immediately. She was also bothered because she didn't feel I heard the argument that she, Danny, and Eric had made. What I did not feel she understood was that I had indeed heard the argument, but I felt there would be a better time to address the issues. That moment should come when the town was not teetering on economic collapse.

I heard a sigh from her side of the bed. I would have rolled my eyes had the room been darker.

"I love you," I said trying to sound as submissive as possible, so at least she would say something.

"I love you Sarah."

"Are you planning on having a conversation with me again?" I asked again, attempting to be meek.

"I am just a little disappointed with how you reacted to everything."

She was "disappointed" I thought to myself. It was that horrible patriarchal term my father used when he was upset with something I had done. It felt like a punch to the gut.

"I'm sorry; I didn't mean to disappoint you." I rolled over with my back to Jill, watching the shadows of the trees outside wave with the wind.

"What Polar Beverage has done, that is a big deal. It was sick and wrong. I understand the town has a great deal on the line and I get that people are scared." Jill's voice was strained. "But you know Sarah; this is the kind of thing, the sort of moral struggle that defines people."

"Jill, these were a bunch of articles off the internet."

With that major linguistic blunder, Jill got up, taking her pillow, and made her way to the couch.

"Jill, I'm sorry."

She said nothing.

We were losing something, maybe passion. In the few short months we had been living together our sex life had dropped to about a third of what it had been before.

Chapter 7

The beginning of August there was a positive energy in Ofiara though, I was feeling cautiously optimistic. It was as though everyone had started to feel confident again, as though Polar Beverage would indeed save us from economic collapse. The building had taken shape and the equipment inside was finally at the point of being installed. No matter how positive things looked, I felt a little like I was waiting for the other shoe to drop.

I didn't feel any more secure when I saw Peter and Douglas again at the City Council meeting that month. Douglas had decided to dress much more formally for this meeting. He was wearing a dress suit without a tie, making him look as though he was on his way to Las Vegas.

I sat in the front with Jill and Eric.

John arrived to his first city council meeting just a minute before it started. I looked at him, puzzled, as he had never expressed the desire to go to a meeting. He gave me a smile and a shrug and then joined his mother who was sitting with Danny in the back of the room.

My dad ran through old business. One woman was there to explain how upset she was that the grass at the park was not being mowed enough. Ester was also present to give her update on the outbreak of stray dogs that had managed to take over the town. Everyone yawned and stretched until she explained that her solution for the problem would be to have Terry simply shoot the dogs.

"Thank you Ester, but I am not sure that is a working solution," my dad responded. He then looked at his sheet of the issues for the evening and motioned Peter forward to the podium.

Peter paused a few moments, making certain he had everyone's attention. "Polar beverage would like to start work on drilling a well. We believe there is a large and ample water source below the factory Polar Beverage currently owns."

Douglas kept his head down; fixated on a piece of paper attached to a clipboard he was holding. Even from three seats away I could hear the occasional sigh coming out of his mouth.

"Initially, we were going to use the city water, but we believe that may be too much of a strain on the current water system." Peter stated with firm confidence.

"What difference will the new well make?" asked Danny from the back of the room.

"Pardon?" asked Peter.

"I am sorry; I meant to ask whether or not you will continue to use the city's water if you build a new well?"

"Do you think there should be concerns?" asked Peter, using the answer a question with a question strategy. He then continued by addressing a grey area. "We are doing this to insure there is no problem."

I knew the conversation would not end well. There was a growing discomfort, the sort of discomfort that comes with an extremely awkward situation like walking in on two people having sex. Or even worse, like walking in on someone masturbating. It was the ugly face of confrontation causing distress within the room, putting our new industry on trial.

"Didn't Polar Water do the same thing in India?" asked Danny. "You know, drill and ask the community later? You know, when it was actually too much later. What sort of an idiot would just drill and ask questions later?"

"That will be enough of that!" my dad said firmly.

"I have no idea what you're talking about," said Peter.

"Are you fucking kidding?" asked Jacqueline. Everyone paused and stared in shock at the French women swearing at a city council meeting.

"I think we all need to settle down a bit," my dad said with a smile, trying to keep neutral in a conversation which was quickly heating up.

Jacqueline stood up. "These guys are going to destroy our town and then they will cut and run. They will not look back and they will not feel guilty."

I could see Douglas out of the corner of my eye. He raised his head and looked at Jacqueline.

"Ok, if we can get some sort of order here," said my dad louder. "The city council, including myself, are all unified in our decision. We feel that the plant is only a benefit to this town. We don't have a choice if we want to economically dig ourselves out of this giant shithole caused by the venting company."

"Is it worth destroying our entire town?" asked Danny loudly.

"All in favor of allowing Polar Beverage to build the well?" my dad asked, ignoring Danny.

Everyone on the council replied, "Yea."

"Everyone opposed?" asked my dad.

None of the council members stated a nay; however, several boos floated from the back of the room.

"Motion passed with one hundred percent support," my dad said with a defiant attitude evident in his voice.

The meeting was adjourned and several of the city council members darted for the side door while my dad stayed and organized his papers. At the very least, my dad was a warrior, that rare person who not only looked forward to confrontations, but sometimes caused them.

Eric walked over to my dad. "There is something that is not right about this, Dad."

"You need to keep your friends under control there Eric," because all they are going to do is cause Polar Beverage to leave and then the whole town will be fucked. Do you want the town to go into the shitter, Eric?" my dad asked in a stern and angry tone. I was looking the other way. I didn't dare to look at either of them; I did not want to fuel the fire by letting either one of them know they had an audience.

Jill walked back to sit with Danny. I turned around and saw Peter standing just a foot from me, looking at me, eye to eye. It was like looking the devil straight in the eyes, the proof of which was the hair on the back of my neck standing up. Regardless of my attempts to remain neutral there were pushes from both sides.

"I think it is awesome that you and your partner have both decided to live together." Peter smiled with his set of oversized teeth. "I hope that the town continues to be accepting of your non-traditional relationship. When I was your age, people kept this sort of thing to themselves."

"What?" I asked not even completely clear on what he said. I had never even spoken to him. I wasn't sure if he was a lunatic or just being a jerk.

A moment later my dad walked over and shook Peter's hand. Everything, every part of this, was so unsettling.

"Sorry about that," my dad said looking over at Peter.

"Not a problem, Donald. There are some people who are just afraid of change."

"Oh Danny means well, but she has some mental health issues." My dad looked around; I assumed to make sure the subject of the conversation was out of earshot. "Sometimes she just doesn't know what she is saying."

"I hope she will not be a problem. If this Danny were to create obstacles, Polar Beverage and the town could face consequences." Peter paused and looked over at me. "It just takes one rotten apple."

Leaving the meeting that night, I called Peter a plethora of names in my head. It would be a while before I was able to voice what I was feeling.

Chapter 8

Eric and I arrived at the police station at two in the morning. He had roused me out of bed about midnight to tell me that Danny had called him in a panic. She had been arrested for drug sales. Her story was that Terry had pulled her over and found fifty grams of methamphetamine in her car. We all knew that Danny sometimes dealt pot but as far as harder drugs, she was strictly hands-off.

The police said we couldn't bail her out until her court hearing on Monday. They did, however, let us visit with her in an open area where we were separated from Danny by a sheet of dirty glass. The room smelled like cleaning fluid, however it looked as though no such product had been used in weeks.

When she sat down it was clear she had been crying since the arrest. Her eyes were red and she was shaking. She only had a few weeks left of her probation and now found herself back in jail. She knew that if she were convicted she was going away for a long time.

"What the hell happened?" asked Eric in a whisper.

"I have no fucking idea. I was driving home from Eric's and Terry pulled me over," Danny stated, looking down and crying again. "I wasn't even drinking and she told me to get out of the car. Then she turned to me and asked 'What is that on your floor?' And before I knew it she leaned over and she had a bag full of meth. I told her I had no idea how it got there. She pulled me out of the car and threw me on the ground and handcuffed me. She didn't even read me my rights."

"How did the meth get in your car?" I asked.

"I don't fucking know." Danny said with her mouth hanging slightly open, "You both know I didn't do this."

"I know," Eric said, touching the glass with one hand. "I believe you and so does Sarah."

I nodded in agreement.

"We can't get you out until Monday, that is the soonest you can get into court." I said sympathetically.

"I know, they already told me." Danny started to sob again. "Thank you."

"Always here for you, Danny," said Eric.

"We have to get you a lawyer," I said.

Danny nodded, touching the glass on one side and Eric touching the other side. It didn't occur to me until that moment that Danny and Eric were more than friends. I realized they were in love. Moreover, I believe that they realized they were in love. It was one of those moments where something beautiful comes out of an ugly moment.

Chapter 9

A pile of past due accounts at the store had been calling me for weeks. It was something I knew I should have organized earlier, but it seemed so much easier to procrastinate. Unfortunately, putting off the task was no longer an option. I had to at least attempt an assessment of how the store was doing financially and get a clear view of how much was owed. Even though a few people had paid off their store credit, about twenty had almost maxed out their credit. It added up to thousands of dollars in unpaid bills.

Selfishly, I was thinking about my future. Trusting some outside corporation seemed like a leap of faith that was just too great. There was a part of me wanted to say to my dad, 'I hope this Polar thing works. If not we are all screwed.' The reality was I would never challenge my dad. It would take nothing less than a miracle or divine epiphany for me to question him. He had a way of shutting people down like he did with Ester and Jacqueline. If he didn't like what I said, he would half listen. The few parts heard would be the ones which supported his argument. When he dug his heels into an idea or argument, getting him to see the other side was almost impossible.

News in town had quickly spread about the big drug bust the previous Friday. Danny no longer had the anonymity which came with dealing a drug like pot. Her recent incarceration brought with it the stigma of being a meth dealer. On the Ofiara social scale, a methamphetamine dealer was maybe a half step above being a pedophile.

Just before leaving, I walked upstairs to talk with Dean. He was wearing a white dress shirt and tie. At age sixty five, he looked as though he could take down a deer with his bare hands. Dean was a retired military officer who worked as a cashier mainly because it kept him busy. He didn't like to golf, or fish, or even to do lawn work. He always told me he had tried all of those "cliché retirement activities" and decided they were things people did only when they had nothing else to do.

"Did you hear about the drug bust last night?" a young woman asked while paying for a twelve pack of Diet Venin. She was obviously headed for the beach in her bikini top and shorts.

Dean looked at her critically, as though he was hoping she would have some sort of further thought on the subject. "What about it?" He asked.

"I heard the deputy confiscated seven hundred grams of meth and several pounds of pot," she replied with mystery in her voice.

"That seems like it would be a lot," Dean replied with the critical look still fixated in his expression.

"Yes, they say it is the biggest drug bust ever in the county," she replied with wide eyes.

"Yeah, I don't know much about drugs and how to measure them. How did you get to know so much about that?" Dean asked.

"Well," replied the young woman. After about a half second she realized Dean was not asking because he was interested but because he thought she was being stupid.

In my head I was silently cheering on Dean.

"You better get down to the beach and join your friends there. Enjoy a nice narcotic-free afternoon," Dean said with a smile.

I smiled at Dean. "I'm heading over to my dad's for dinner."

"Let me tell you a secret Sarah." He leaned towards me. "I hate teenagers. Not just a little, a great deal."

I smiled and said, "I know that, Dean."

"I'm a teenager," Jason said from somewhere a few aisles away.

"Jason is an elderly woman in a young man's body. I am waiting for him to come in one day smelling like muscle rub," Dean said, with a devilish grin.

"I can actually hear you, Dean!" Jason shouted.

"If you two need anything, call," I said on my way out the door.

There was a heavy tension in the air at my parent's house, a prelude to something bad. I could feel it the moment I walked through the front door. I hoped it was something which would simply pass or that everyone could overlook it long enough to eat dinner.

Jill was in the kitchen helping my mom.

"Sarah," my mom said.

"Hi Mom."

"Hello," Jill said as she walked to the door and kissed me. Although I kissed her back, the public display made me uncomfortable. It wouldn't have mattered if I was a heterosexual or homosexual, I didn't like that sort of thing.

"Sarah, can you set the table?" my mom asked.

"Yes Mom."

I grabbed a stack of plates and silverware on my way to the backyard. Eric arrived just after I walked outside. He looked like an old rag, tired and stressed out. I'm sure Danny being in jail was difficult for him. Without saying anything, he gave me a half smile and walked into the house.

I started setting the picnic table when Douglas walked around the side of the house with two bottles of wine.

"Hey Douglas," I said, almost in the form of a question, but I did not want to be rude.

"Your dad invited me for dinner," he said, alleviating my confusion.

"Well, pull up a seat," I responded. "Can I get you something to drink?"

"Not right now, thank you," Douglas answered.

Eric and Jill walked into the backyard, both carrying large plates of food.

The next person to emerge from the front was my dad. He carried a large plate filled with some sort of meat.

"Douglas," He said warmly. "Welcome!"

We all sat down at the table. Immediately, everyone started to fill their plates with food.

Just then, John arrived.

"You're late," announced my dad.

"Sorry, I was at the jail in Grand Rapids visiting a friend. A priest's collar can get a person into any building in the country." John scooped up some potato salad and dropped it onto his plate as he sat down.

"Yeah, especially prison, they let them right in," Eric said, attempting to make a joke to lighten the moment.

"Don't go there, Eric," my mom said, taking a seat next to my dad.

"How is Danny doing?" I asked John.

"Well, still scared but I think better."

Jill was poking a piece of mystery meat with a fork, as if she felt the force could reanimate it.

"I hope like hell you aren't also implicated in that crap, Eric," my dad said.

"I wasn't selling it and for that matter she wasn't selling it." Eric said assertively.

"OK, are we done talking about this?" My mom asked.

Eric looked at my mom like a deer in the headlights.

"Let's at least wait until dinner is over," my mom said with a smile. She always said that the biggest thing she learned from years of singing in bars and restaurants was that you could say anything with a smile and people would listen.

My dad rolled his eyes and Eric looked at me as though he was going to pop.

"Danny wouldn't sell meth," I said in a low, under the radar sort of way.

My mom cleared her throat "Douglas, welcome to our home."

"Thank you, Mrs. Polsky."

My mom had successfully changed the subject. "Can I ask where you grew up?"

"Actually, I grew up in Granite Lakes, a few hours southwest of here," Douglas said, grabbing another piece of meat off the large tray with his fork.

"I know the area fairly well. I used to work at a resort there in the summer. It was when I was working my way through college." My mom smiled and took a drink of her wine. "What part of town did you live in?"

"Birch Bark Trailer Park."

"Interesting place," my mom said, raising one eyebrow.

"It is not as bad as everyone says," Douglas laughed and looked around the table.

"It has a reputation for being a rough place," said my mom with a polite smile. She then said in a whisper, "Drugs."

Douglas smiled like he was trying to hold something back. "Actually, there was only one drug bust that I know of and that was my uncle Frank. He lived next door to us in the park. He got caught growing pot. He got a few months in jail."

"Sounds difficult," John said, with a tone of concern.

"It wasn't bad. I was quite happy."

"Do your parents still live there?" asked my mom, taking a bit of salad.

"Well," he smiled, "my parents divorced when I was very young. I grew up with my mom. She still lives in the trailer park."

"I'm sorry to hear that, Douglas."

Douglas got a puzzled look on his face. It was though he was trying to figure out why my mom was sorry.

"Where did you go to college?" I asked.

"Augsburg."

"Business major?" asked my dad, looking over at Eric.

"Actually, no," said Douglas.

"What then?" asked Eric, looking over at our dad with a smug look.

"Geology and my Master of Science is in Environmental Studies."

Eric and I looked at each other and then went back to our food, both of us trying to hold back a laugh.

"What did you do before you got to Polar Beverage?" I asked with increasing curiosity.

"When I'll tell you; however, I'm guessing that you wouldn't believe me," said Douglas, pausing and looking around the table. "I worked for environmental group."

"It all seems so innocent," Jill whispered with her mouth covered.

My dad choked a little on his food. "Really? What brought you to Polar?"

"Peter did, actually. He recruited me after I and a group of other activists hung a giant sign off a bridge to let people know we did not agree with some of the things Polar Beverage was doing."

"What could possibly make you change your mind?" Eric asked almost irritated.

"Because I felt as though I could do something good. Peter said working for Polar would be a chance for me to change things," replied Douglas, looking straight at Eric.

"Are you achieving that goal?" Jill asked.

Douglas smiled and laughed but did not answer the question.

"How's the money?" Eric asked.

"Good," Douglas replied without giving a number.

"So, Douglas, how long is Peter in town for? When is he going to release the reins on you and let you run the plant?" asked my dad, in an attempt to change the subject.

"He's going to be here three, maybe four months. After that he will go back to Chicago with visits every six months," Douglas answered, looking down.

Peter was staying at Spring Hill, a resort on the other side of the lake. The resort was one of the nicest in Minnesota. It was unlikely that anyone from town would ever go there unless it was for work. They hired a few locals, including my mother, but they mainly employed happy, perky, and chipper college kids. Young men and women who fit into a specific image of being clean, polite, and beautiful.

After dinner, Jill went into the house with my mom and my father disappeared with his litany of Sunday calls. This left John, Eric, and I with Douglas cleaning off the table. We all silently went about our work until Douglas spoke.

"I have the number for a very good lawyer out of Minneapolis," Douglas said as he opened his wallet and fished something out. He handed a card to Eric.

John looked skeptically at Douglas while Eric took the card and looked at it

"Danny needs one," said Douglas. "Please say thank you to your mom."

I nodded towards him and he walked towards the street.

Walking home later that afternoon, Jill and I stopped at the store to make sure everything was under control, and of course it was. Dean was counting out the money in the cash register and getting ready to close up.

As we walked out of the store I looked over and saw Eric's truck in Jacqueline's driveway.

"Well, that's a bit strange," I said, looking over at Jill.

Jill walked back into the store. A few minutes later she came back outside with a small bunch of daisies from the store.

"For me?" I asked

"Nope," she smiled. "I really want to meet her."

"Who?" I asked.

"Jacqueline," Jill said, hesitating, knowing I really wasn't in the mood for a visit.

"Dean just gave you those flowers without paying, didn't he?" I asked.

"Yep," Jill responded, walking towards the house.

I sighed, "OK." This wasn't really on my list of things I wanted to do that day, but it seemed to be important to Jill that she meet Jacqueline.

"Come on, let's go."

We knocked on the door and Jake answered.

"Hello," I said.

"Jill, come in." said Jake.

"Excuse me?" I said

"Yeah, you too," Jake said.

We walked through the kitchen then to a large living room. Jacqueline always had several plants and overstuffed earth toned furniture. When John and I were growing up, we usually ended up at his house. The truth was, Jacqueline let us get away with more stuff than my mom did.

Jacqueline was sitting on a large green chair, with Todd and Eric sitting on a sofa. There was that awkward silence of a newcomer entering. Jacqueline stood up.

"Sarah," she said warmly.

"This is Jill," I said.

"We brought some flowers." Jill said to Jacqueline.

"Thank you," said Jacqueline taking the flowers. "Please sit."

Jill and I sat on a loveseat opposite the room from Todd and Eric. Jake sat on the arm of the loveseat next to Jill.

"We were just talking about Danny's arrest," Todd said.

"We are talking about why Danny would have been targeted," Jake replied bluntly.

"I am not sure if I am stating the obvious here, but did anyone here know that counties which have increased drug issues get more funding from the state?" Todd said. If anyone in the room would know something like this, it would be Todd. His father had been a cop in Duluth for close to 40 years.

"I don't doubt that was the reason behind this, but why Danny? Danny may have done other things, but she would not make or distribute a drug like meth." Eric said a little irritated.

"I think it was because of what she said at the city council meeting." Jacqueline replied.

"Really?" I asked pessimistically.

"This is very common," Jacqueline said, taking a drink out of a tall glass of water.

"I think we are all wandering into Jimmy Hoffa territory." I said.

"What Terry did is a diversion. It is like a thief burning down a barn so that a farmer does not see him stealing the horses."

I knew the conversation was steering back into Polar Beverage conspiracy theory. Not only was I skeptical, I honestly I was tired of only hearing the negative about what was going on. The beverage company was hope for the town and hope for my store. The idea of the company moving into town meant I could maybe make enough money to do better than just break even every month. I felt like the company was being sabotaged before they even had a chance. In my mind it seemed like the easy route, rather than just calling Terry out.

"Seriously, I don't think any of this is really helping Danny," I said. "Perhaps we should be focusing more on just getting her out of jail and confronting Terry?"

"It is a quick fix," Jacqueline said.

"It's realistic," I retorted.

"Sarah, I watched you grow up and I taught you in high school. I know you are smart. But, you must always remember that the devil shits in the same place twice."

I did not quite understand what she meant. "Sorry?"

"What I mean is that if it happened once, it will happen again. This is not anything new to Polar Beverage. Not only will it happen again, but things will get worse," Jacqueline replied.

"Well, when there is a reason, if something salient happens, then we can do something. We can get a lawyer or tell the police. What we are doing now seems counterproductive," I said a little defensively.

Jacqueline looked around then looked at me. "Let me ask you a question Sarah; what if Polar Beverage does damage the town's water system?"

"Polar will be the ones to pay," I responded.

"How is this going to happen?" Jacqueline asked, waiting for a response. She then went on. "There is no law on the state books which would allow us to take action against a company which took water from a well. There are laws about lakes and wetlands. There are also laws about pollution and contaminating water systems, but again, there is no law specifically meant to protect what is underground. They have the same right to the water system as we do."

"So, it is kind of like fucking a girl without a condom," replied Jake taking a drink of tea and then looked up to see everyone was staring at him.

"Nice, Jake," I said sarcastically.

"Ah yeah, thank you for that colorful description Jake," Todd said with a look of annoyance.

"I think the point is that if something should happen to the water supply we are shit out of luck," Eric said with a smile.

"Ok, I think we are getting a little ahead of ourselves." I looked over at Jill for an affirmation of sanity, "Don't you think?"

Jill gave a half smile and shrugged.

Chapter 10

Danny's court hearing had been set for 9:30am on the Monday following her arrest. Todd, Jake, Eric and I sat patiently for several hours before her case was heard. Every few minutes, I would look over and glare at Terry, who was sitting at the back of the room.

Danny's mother was also in court that morning. She didn't look at any of us or say a word. I didn't know her that well, but I felt there was a clear stream of animosity coming in our direction. It seemed as though she blamed Eric for the legal issues Danny already had and it was likely she also, at least on some level, blamed Eric for the meth bust.

John walked in late wearing his collar. He whispered, "Hey, sorry I am late." He sat down on the bench behind us. "I could have told you this wasn't going to start on time."

"Shush," Jake whispered.

"Is Danny's lawyer here?" asked John.

"Yep," Todd whispered. "See that scary demon-looking woman?" He pointed to his right. "If I were facing jail time, I would want her to represent me."

John looked over to see Janis Manson, who was no relation to Charles but looked twice as scary. She did not need the swastika on her head. Instead, she wore a black dress suit, white shirt, and a gray tie. Her dark hair was pulled back into a tight ponytail. If all of this wasn't intimidating enough, she must have been six feet tall, without her heels, which added about four inches. There was something very sexy about her.

"I wonder if she is dating anyone." Jake said, raising his eyebrows.

Todd looked over at Jake and responded "What the hell Jake? Why do you have to talk like that?"

Danny's case was called and she shuffled in wearing handcuffs. With file and briefcase in hand, Janis walked to one of the two tables just past the gallery seats. She stood there as a woman's voice demanded that everyone rise.

"We are here today to decide on bail for Ms. Danny Anderson," said a stuffy grey-haired man who sat in the judge's chair.

A middle-aged, overweight man asked if he could approach the bench. He handed a file to the judge. "The people request a bail of twenty thousand dollars."

"Ouch," I mumbled. "Shit."

"How exactly do you justify a bail so high?" asked Janis in a monotone voice.

"Well, first because she has a prior conviction and second, because she had 50 grams of meth with intention to sell," the prosecutor said.

"How exactly are you going to prove the meth belonged to Ms. Anderson?" asked Janis.

"It was found in her car," stated the prosecutor.

"There were no fingerprints found on the bag. Additionally, there was no meth found in her system, and no meth whatsoever found in her home. It sounds to me like you have a relatively weak case for someone requesting a whopping twenty thousand dollar bail." Janis did not even look up from her paperwork as she said this. It was clear she had flustered the prosecutor. She was calling his bluff as an outsider within a very closed off legal community. In northern Minnesota it was common for overworked attorneys, both defense and prosecution, to make deals with one another. Janis did not look like the type who was good at making a deal. She looked like the type that would win.

"We would be willing to drop the bail to fifteen thousand." said the prosecution.

"OK, I would love to sit here all day and listen to you two haggle, but we have ten other cases to see before the end of the day," the judge stated. "Bail is set at five thousand dollars."

Following a plethora of paperwork, bureaucracy, and more money than any of us could afford, we were all headed out of an overly crowded courthouse parking lot. I could see Terry on the street next to her sheriff's car. She was looking at her wheels.

I regretted riding with Jake as we inched past Terry. The deputy was standing on the road still looking at the side of her cruiser. It wasn't until we were right next to her car I realized the two driver's side tires were flat.

"Oh great," I said with an exhausted sigh.

Overall, Danny's luck was less than desirable. A letter in the mail that day informed her that she did not have a job at the new plant. It was ironic that she took such issue with the corporation but did not seem to see a problem working for them. It also could have been she did not have much of a choice.

Later that afternoon, Eric received a call letting him know he got the same job for which Danny had been rejected. The one advantage Eric had over Danny was the same that he had over all the applicants: our father. He was one of the strongest forces behind getting Polar Beverage into Ofiara, and had campaigned quite hard to ensure Eric had a job at the beverage company when the venting plant closed.

In total, fifty calls went out that day to different people in town and the surrounding area. Peter called all his new employees, letting them know they would start training next week. His plan was for the plant to formally start production between the end of August and the beginning of September.

Since the beverage plant had been approved by council, Peter had been diligently working towards getting to get to know the community. He came into the grocery store at least twice a week and ordered specialty, usually expensive, items. He was also a frequent customer at the restaurant next door. He would sit and talk with the regulars for hours, it didn't matter who. I felt he was trying to understand the dynamics of the town, dissect, and pull things apart.

The thing is people loved talking to Peter. He was a symbol of that wealthy corporate world which did not seem to care what small town people thought. Peter was the closest thing most of the community members would get to a world so different and so beyond their reach. He was a superhero, movie star, and politician all rolled into one neat and expensive package. People loved him. Well, people that were not part of a small group which had formed to plan the downfall of Polar Beverage.

The biggest thing Peter did was to make our town feel like Ofiara had a future. When he made the phone calls that day, it was like lifejackets being thrown to people who were exhausted from treading water. It was like he was the answer to many prayers.

Chapter 11

By mid August, Jason and I were getting tired of spending most of the day inside. It seemed like the entire world was out enjoying the nice weather except us. This didn't seem very fair. We decided to set up chairs outside and take turns going inside and helping individuals wanting to pay for their groceries. I saw this as one of the benefits of being self-employed.

Monet walked over and sat between the two chairs, looking washed and regal. It appeared my cousin was taking good care of him. Jason fed the dog from a plastic bag of dog snacks he bought from the store.

The one thing I had not anticipated was that the smell drifting up from the lake would make us want to be at the beach even more.

Jason grinned from behind his sunglasses, "Maybe we could talk John into switching buildings with us. We could take the church and be almost right on the lake."

I smiled, putting my sunglasses on. "Yes, I think you should bring that up next time you see him. Test the waters on that one."

"Yes," Jason said intensely. "I'll do that."

My dad walked out of the city hall building and crossed the street. He didn't seem to be taking the summer heat well and had a small stain of sweat on his white dress shirt. "Sarah, this doesn't look very professional."

"It's fine Dad. It's Monday, there's no one around," I said, looking up at him. I was a little hurt by his disapproval and the notion that he felt it was any of his business.

"It just looks a little sloppy, like you really don't care about the customers," my dad said looking around like someone from the Better Business Bureau was going to jump out and throw a fine at me.

"Dad! Stop, please!"

"I have to agree Sarah, this does look bad," Jason said, placing a treat between his lips and letting Monet grab it with his own mouth.

"I am not sure I recall asking your opinion. What I recall is you getting excited about the idea of sitting outside," I said with a sour smile.

Jason smiled back and shrugged.

"Did you get that dog registered yet?" my dad asked Jason.

"Well," Jason stretched back. "Registration would imply I am the owner, and I am not sure Monet wants to be owned. Perhaps that is why he ran away from his first family, because they claimed ownership over him."

"Or, maybe they dumped his hairy ass off on the edge of the woods because they were sick of him." My father was getting annoyed. "Is he registered?"

"Yes, last week. I haven't put the tag on yet," Jason said.

"Well, you better take care of him. Ester is on the war path because of the strays in town. I keep getting angry calls from her, saying that the dogs are running everywhere and getting into her flowerbed," my dad replied.

"I don't think I've seen any other strays, Dad."

"Well, I'm not sure why she would lie?" my dad responded skeptically.

"I don't think she was lying, Dad..."

Jason cut in. "I'm with Ester, Uncle Don. I can see it. They are coming into town, expecting a free meal then they sleep right in our backyards. Freeloading good-for-nothings. We need to round them up and put them in a big cage."

"Yes," my dad responded even though he knew full well Jason was being sarcastic.

"Uncle Don, Monet does not like to be inside. If I cage him up I am doing it against his will." Jason responded.

"It's a damn dog, Jason," my dad responded.

"Don, he has thoughts and feelings. He can feel love as well as hate. He can sense danger and if someone gets angry at him, he feels fear. I would say he is very much like us." Jason was now matching my father's irritation.

"I don't find this funny, Jason."

"Don, I'm not trying to be funny. I love you very much, but with all due respect, I think Ester is just being stupid and dragging others into her stupidity."

"I am heading home." My dad grunted and walked off.

Jake pulled up in his Mustang. He jumped out of the car and ran inside giving us a small wave. I slowly followed him into the store. I was half hoping Jason would volunteer to help Jake, but that didn't happen.

"Hey there," Jake said with a smile, walking back to the produce section.

"Jake, did you have anything to do with the flat tires on a deputy's car?" I asked.

I heard a giggle come from his direction on the other side of the store.

Walking back up to the counter, he smiled and tried to look clever. "No, what happened?"

"Jake, I know you meant well, but really, this is just bringing more attention to Danny and it could have a negative impact."

"I disagree. I think that Terry needs to be sent a message," said Jake. "She's been getting away with this kind of shit for years."

"You know, you guys are acting like children. Do you really think what you are doing is helping the situation?" I asked skeptically.

"No, I don't, but I am not just going to bend over and take it," Jake responded, taking his produce and walking out the door.

"It's not really your fight though, Jake." I said. The words created a defensive look on his face like he was irritated with me.

Although a large part of me felt he had a very valid point, there was also that part of me that so afraid of what might happen. It's that fear that filled me, preventing me from making huge change because that change might make me stand out. It was the fear that I would become the focus of someone's anger.

Chapter 12

The warm winds of mid-August took their time dragging through Ofiara. There was a stagnant heat which seemed to slow everything in a sort of suspended animation. It was just too hot to do anything. Our town smelled of dust with the occasional lawn cutting creating a welcome grass smell.

With the completion of the Polar bottling plant, many families within the community were looking forward to seeing a pay check again. In fact, this foundation of hopefulness had paved the road for at least three families to pay off their tabs at the grocery store. However, there remained a healthy amount of skepticism regarding the beverage company. The comments Danny had made at the city council meeting continued to float around town. They were accusations that had left the seed of doubt in the minds of several residents.

The only thing that dismantled negative thoughts of Polar's intentions was the person doing the discrediting. Danny continued to be perceived as a meth dealer. She was now considered to be an outsider, bringing in addiction and death. Because of her current standing in town, most individuals did not consider her to be a reliable source. In fact, most people thought Danny was a creep.

Regardless of any negative perceptions training had started at the bottling plant. There were groups of men, and a few women, coming and going from the plant all day. The workers had to learn an entirely new system. A small part of me was jealous that the workers got to be a part of something so new, so interesting, and so not the world of groceries.

Strange things started to happen to the town's water with the machinery at the plant working. There were strange noises, like air bubbles in the pipes. People coming into the store would talk about the loud banging sounds when they turned the water in their homes on and off. It sounded the same as when the utilities department is working on a water line.

Noises in the pipes were the least of my issues. I no longer had a desire to go to work. Every month the profit margin seemed to be slightly smaller. Work was becoming an emotionally destructive force, too overwhelming to try and change. I would sit in my office in the basement of the store and trudge though past due tabs from several members of the community. I would like to say that some altruistic part of me looked upon the overdue tabs as my contribution towards the struggles of the community. Quite frankly I resented being in that position. The way things were headed it looked as though my retirement was going to be a dream. Giving up the things I wanted because someone else could not pay their bills was unfair.

The thing was, making the store work really wasn't a choice. Aside from myself, I employed three people. I wasn't able to offer much in the way of benefits. I was able to give a relatively large bonus around Christmas time and I created a small 401k plan, but health insurance was well beyond my budget.

As I walked upstairs from the office, I told myself to let things go and have a good day. The alternative was frustration eating me alive. Just as I had used self-talk to reassure myself everything would be better, the pipes started to moan, followed by a scratching sound running throughout the basement. I jumped.

"Damn it," I muttered as I reached the top of the stairs.

"Hey Sarah, sorry about that," Norma said, without even looking back at me.

"Norma, it wasn't your fault," I said with a laugh.

Norma was filling a bucket on wheels with water and a very powerful lemon scented cleaner. She was always so focused on keeping the store clean. She was constantly washing the floor, the windows, counters, and shelves. She said once a clean and organized environment made her feel productive.

Through the front window, I could see Eric walking towards the store. The white t-shirt he was wearing was stained with gray and black marks. His jeans had that same wear and tear on them.

"How was your first day?" I asked as he walked through the door.

"It was ok," he said looking around. "Hey Norma." he said giving a smile and a wave to the woman with the bucket.

"What's up?" I asked, a little puzzled, as Eric seemed almost detached. There was a look on his face, like he was worried but did not know quite what it was that he was worried about.

"Can we talk?" Eric asked.

"Yeah," I said grabbing a pack of cigarettes for Eric and motioning for him to follow me towards the back entrance.

"Don't forget to pay for those," Norma reminded me. I had put her in charge of inventory because she was the pickiest person I knew. If anything was missing, she would find it.

When Eric and I reached the alley, I handed him the cigarettes.

"Thanks Sis."

I smiled. "You are going to pay me back, someday."

"I saw something strange today," Eric said, opening the pack and pulling out a cigarette.

"Like what?"

"I don't really know how to describe it," he said as he placed the white stick to his mouth and lit it. "I'm not even really sure if there is anything wrong."

"Do you intend on telling me today or will this be some guessing game over a few weeks?" I asked with a smile.

"Sarah, I am serious."

"Ok, what's going on?"

"When I got into the plant last night, around eleven pm, Peter was there meeting with Douglas." Eric looked at me and paused. "They looked like they were arguing a little. Then Peter walked out of the meeting and gathered everyone for an announcement."

"And?" I smiled. I would get slightly annoyed when Eric would take a long time to tell a story. "Did magic rainbow monkeys fly out of his ass?"

Eric gave me a slight glare which communicated his need to finish the story. "OK, this is going to sound strange, but he promoted two people to shift supervisors."

"Well, seems normal. You especially need a supervisor."

"No, what was strange was who was promoted. Douglas announced it would be Juan Suarez and Sam Andrews."

I looked at my brother, a little shocked. This seemed like a stupid decision. There was a history between the two men which was at the very least adversarial.

Juan's parents had moved to Ofiara when he was in third grade, because his father got a job as a human resources manager at In-House. Juan and Sam became good friends in grade school. They were like kindred spirits, and up into high school they were almost always together.

No one knows the exact moment the exchange took place; it was some time in their senior year of high school. Some people say it was after track practice, while others claimed Sam and Juan were at a party. Whatever had happened, it was at Sam who dropped the S bomb and called Juan a "fucking spick." Neither one of them seemed to ever get past the fact Sam had used that word.

"Why do you think Douglas would do that?" I asked. Neither one of them was qualified to run the plant. Sam was organized, but he was often quick to anger. Juan was smart, but would often mix things up, lacking anything resembling organizational skills.

"I have no damn idea," Eric replied. "What I do know is that three of the managers from In-House are working at the Polar plant and not one of them was promoted to supervisor." Eric subtly dropped his cigarette on the ground.

"It does seem strange," I said, picking up Eric's cigarette butt.

Chapter 13

At the end of August there were two more drug busts, at least one of which was legitimate. Unfortunately, legitimacy did not matter in Ofiara. Instead, it was the perception of legitimacy.

The first drug bust involved Terry simply knocking on Jacqueline's front door. The retired teacher opened the door and the deputy saw Jacqueline stoned, with a baggie filled with marijuana on her kitchen counter. Terry then arrested Jacqueline, on the spot, for being under the influence of an illegal substance. Later, Terry added a charge of intent to sell her stash. Apparently, her prescription for medicinal marijuana had expired.

The second arrest was of a man named Franklin Jackson. He didn't grow up in Ofiara or any of the surrounding communities. Franklin was from Minneapolis, and since he was from out of town, he was seen as less trustworthy than the locals. Franklin had been in the store several times. On one of his shopping trips he told me his family had moved to Ofiara so he could work on his doctoral dissertation on sustainable farming.

Franklin was arrested only a few days after Jacqueline, but required six times the law enforcement needed for Jacqueline's arrest. People driving past said they saw ten to twenty police cars between his farmhouse and barn. The charges were something to the effect that he was connected with the methamphetamine production. The rumor the following day was that officers had found massive amounts of chemicals used to make meth in the barn.

Chapter 14

John and I drove to his mother's bail hearing together. He was terrified his mother would end up serving the rest of her life in jail. Although I didn't think they were going to throw the book at Jacqueline, I didn't want John to feel I was invalidating his fears by telling him "It's OK."

The jail staff seemed to be very respectful of Jacqueline and she returned that respect. However, it was still excruciatingly difficult to see her in handcuffs. I felt that same flood of emotion a person might feel if they had seen someone being pulled out of a car with a serious injury, weak and helpless. It was uncomfortable and I just wanted to be able to do something. No matter how difficult it was for me, it had to be a thousand times harder for John.

I looked over at Terry who was across the room, on the side of the prosecutor. She sat there, her face void of any emotion. The deputy filled her seat no differently than a purse. I could see nothing there until I realized that was the problem. She was not able to look at Jacqueline.

Although Jacqueline had an attorney, Danny's lawyer, Janis, had shown up and was sitting in the back of the court room. She was watching like a cat ready to pounce, waiting for a mistake.

"What the hell is Danny's attorney doing here?" I whispered.

John looked over and shrugged. His mind was on an issue which was much more immediate.

The same stagnant older judge who had presided over Danny's hearing entered the courtroom. I wondered for a moment if they put him away in a cryogenic chamber between trials.

"In the case of the people versus Jacqueline Collin on the charges of being under the influence of a controlled substance, how do you plead?" the judge asked.

"Guilty, Your Honor." Jacqueline said this without giving her attorney a chance to speak.

The judge looked inquisitively at Jacqueline. "Ok, how do you plead on the charges of possession of a controlled substance?"

"Again, I am guilty Your Honor," Jacqueline said in a very matter of fact tone.

The judge looked a little taken back. "And how do you plead on the charges of intention to distribute a controlled substance?" The judge asked, looking intently for her response.

"OK, that one I am not guilty," Jacqueline said, shaking her head.

The prosecutor spoke up. "Your Honor, we are recommending a ten thousand dollar bail and that Jacqueline willingly turn over her passport. Much of her family is living in Quebec and we believe she is a significant flight risk."

"Are you serious?" asked Jacqueline. "I am a retired woman on a fixed income. Most of my close relatives in Canada are dead. The ones that are alive I don't care so much for. So, you see I am no flight risk, Mr. Liar."

"Excuse me? Liar?" said the prosecutor.

John and I had to bite out tongues and hold our laughter at bay. We knew a full on giggle would only serve to damage Jacqueline's case.

Jacqueline's attorney quickly cut in. "Your Honor, sometimes Ms. Collin's English is not so good. That is how she pronounces lawyer."

"Yes, that is it." Jacqueline said looking at the prosecutor with a glare.

"I'm letting Ms. Collin go without bail under the assumption we will have no trouble getting her back for trial," the judge said.

A bailiff walked with Jacqueline to the back of the courtroom and took her handcuffs off. Smiling at her, he said in a low voice, "I hope this goes well for you Jacqueline. It was a pleasure meeting you."

"Thank you, same here," she said with class.

Terry was making her way out the door and Jacqueline said to her, "You're an old monkey; you need to learn a new trick, this one is getting old."

Terry looked at John. In return he offered her a look of disgust.

John and Jacqueline dropped me off at my house when we got back to Ofiara. I needed a little change of pace and curiosity was killing me. I peeked over the fence, looking at Douglas' backyard to see what he had done with the place.

He had planted daisies and wildflowers all around a path which led to an open area in the trees. There was a table and chair set in the opening of all the greenery. There were pots and soil all along the house as though he was starting plants for the following year.

"You like it?" said a man's voice behind me, making me jump.

I turned around and smiled at Douglas holding two fishing rods. "I love it. You've done great. Last year that yard was completely overrun with weeds."

Douglas was dressed much different than usual. He had on a pair of raggedy old cut-offs and a stained t shirt. His hair was pulled back in a bandana.

"I have a bit of a love for plants, although I am not always good at keeping them alive," he said with a laugh.

"Botany isn't my strong suit either." I smiled.

"Hey, I saw Jill leaving with some bags, everything OK? Did you piss her off?"

"Yeah, she has training on some new therapy through the State of Minnesota: she'll be back on Wednesday."

"How about a little fishing?" Douglas asked in his chipper voice. "I have two rods," he said, waving them in front of me.

I ran home and changed my clothes. Then, the two of us then made our way down to the dock in the back of Douglas' house. We set things up at the end of the dock. Douglas took off his shoes and socks and put his feet into the cool water.

"What are we fishing for?" I asked.

"Sunfish, pan fryers." He grinned and put a piece of corn on his hook.

"Corn?" I laughed.

"Oh, you laugh, but there is nothing better. I got a little carton of worms for you, oh doubting one."

With the sun still high in the sky the world seemed peaceful and quiet. I took a moment, staring past the water to the trees and houses on the other side of the lake. A soft breeze blew across the lake.

Douglas placed his line in the water while I was still struggling to get my worm on the hook. A few minutes later there was a visible tug on his line.

"You got one!" I whispered with excitement.

We both stood up as he pulled a one pound sunfish out of the water. He gently pulled the hook out and placed the fish in a small bucket.

"So, Douglas, do you have a wife? Girlfriend? Male companion?"

He laughed. "I have a girlfriend, she is living in Minneapolis. She is still kind of deciding if moving here is what she wants."

"Small town living is definitely not for everyone," I replied, realizing the way I said it was a bit hickish.

"Agreed, but her issue is more with me working for Polar Beverage. She doesn't like Polar in any way, shape, or form."

"Hmmm," I said, finally putting my line into the water.

"The plant is a chance for me to try and change things, to create something that can be both environmentally friendly and economically viable. This is my chance to try and find a better way."

I felt a little like I was on the receiving end of a sales pitch. Really, who was he trying to convince?

"Your girlfriend doesn't believe this can be done?" I asked.

"Nope, she doesn't believe you can create change from the belly of the beast." Douglas placed another piece of corn on his line.

"And you don't think you are corruptible?" I said with a grin.

"Honestly, I think that everyone is corruptible to a point, but for the most part people have good intentions."

"What are you going to do?" I asked, tugging on my fishing line, a little humiliated we were fishing in the same spot and neither one of us was getting anything.

Just after I finished the question I noticed another tug Douglas' line.

He started pulling. "I am going to try and prove her wrong."

"What about Peter? What's his vision?" I asked.

"No idea," Douglas said with a smile.

Chapter 15

In the time since Danny's arrest and her luck had continued to decline. No matter how well people knew her they now saw her as a meth dealer, even the ones who used to buy pot from her. Moreover, she had absolutely no source of income now. She didn't have a job and she couldn't sell pot. If she was caught selling she could be sent to prison for years. Sadly, it was unlikely most people would buy from her anyway as one of the rumors floating around was that she laced her pot with meth.

What scared me was the mentality which seemed to surface when people talked about Danny. Ofiara residents, including my dad, just seemed to get angry when talking about her and what she was accused of doing. When her name was brought up in conversation at the store people would use words such as unforgiveable, sick, and of course irresponsible. She had very much become a target of animosity. I am ashamed to say I didn't do a great deal to help the situation. I didn't defend her name in conversation or try and offer up excuses. Though, in retrospect, I should have said something.

By the onset of September Danny's life looked very bleak. She ended up losing her apartment and moving in with Eric. At least that is what they told everyone. What I actually believed was that Eric and Danny had decided to move in together and used the current tragedy as a cover story. The truth was that in spite of what was going on those around the new couple could see something special was happening.

People didn't seem to care as much about what happened to Jacqueline. The talk and gossip in the grocery store was of the shame of a teacher being arrested for pot. There was no room for weakness or need; thoughts on the issue were simply black or white. It was right or it was wrong. The arrest made her into a caricature and molded in a way in which people could wrap their thoughts around.

The Polar bottling plant was finally up and running. There were red, white, and black trucks coming and going from the plant several times a day. Bringing in raw materials and shipping out bottles of soda.

Additionally, the moaning and banging of the pipes had graduated to a significant drop in water pressure. People talked and complained about it but no one was really up in arms at this point. The town was still at a point where a good pay check was more important than being able to fill their bathtub faster.

Jill looked up from her pancakes "So?" She asked.

"So?" I responded.

"Ok, doesn't it seem odd how Ofiara is just fine with Polar and what they are doing? Even with the water pressure as bad as it is."

"In all fairness Jill, the new plant has helped the town."

"It just seems that people are not really thinking about what could happen. They are only thinking about what is happening at the moment, anything past the here and now doesn't seem to matter."

"I guess I don't really get what you are trying to say." I said even though a part of me did. I got that something could go wrong. In fact, I lived in fear something could go wrong.

"What I am trying to say, in my own so long and drawn out kind of way, is that if people are distracted by issues which seem as though they merit more immediate attention it's likely those people are not going to think about issues which are bigger and seem less immediate. They cannot pull people into the street here and shoot them like they did in South America. But, they can create a venue for which people think about things other than the water pressure."

"Honestly Jill, I am much more worried about the foreclosure list in the newspaper than issues with what might happen with Polar. People are struggling to just to pay their bills. Two more families have left town. They simply abandoned their homes and left." I said a little snottier than I meant to.

"People get tired of struggling." Jill stated.

"Yeah, I get tired of struggling also." I said. "I haven't just left town in the middle of the night."

"What else are they supposed to do?" Jill said.

"Why do people not even try to wait it out?" I asked "I know you don't agree but this really does seem to me like a cut and run mentality. It is just heartbreaking people would give up."

"I don't think it's that easy, people see this as a fight they cannot win. And, what exactly is it that the town gave to them?"

"Well, for starters the town gave or gives a sense of community." I stated with pride.

"Yes, for the business owners and those who are financially secure?"

"Oh come on." I said defensively.

Jill was trying hard to make me understand her viewpoint. "I could see that as true for those individuals who are in power, you know the ones who understand what is going on. But, what about the guy who is watching his family lose everything and he feels helpless to do anything? What about the guys who were laid off from In-House and didn't get hired by Polar."

"They have a voice Jill, and they also have the ability to change and evolve. They can go back to school or find another job. Opportunity is never going to fall into the lap of the guy sitting in his house waiting for the world to save him."

"So it is up to the individual to change what is happening to them?" Jill asked with a half grin.

"Yes, it's individual ingenuity. How well you do is contingent on how hard you are willing to work."

"So then, again, they really don't owe to the community which basically tells them in times of tragedy they are on their own? It's my understanding that prior to these families leaving they had been listed under foreclosures in the paper for quite some time. The community had more than ample time to do something to help them."

"Ok, I see your point, but just so you know, I don't agree with you."

Jill looked at me disapprovingly.

"Hey, there is a letter from that Franklin guy in the editorial section of the paper." I said looking at Jill and handing her the paper.

To the Editor:

Last spring my wife and our two children decided to sell our home and move to a small farm on the outskirts of Ofiara. We were very excited to make this move as both my wife and I grew up in small towns. This was a gamble; we knew that and understood the risks. I left a job as a professor at the University of Minnesota to come here and make this place home.

It was exciting to see how nice the people of Ofiara were. We felt at home and really thought that this would be the place we would retire. Then, a few weeks ago a deputy came out to our house with a search warrant, which at the very least had no merit. What she found was farm chemicals which had been left over from the previous owner.

For those of you who have never been arrested or falsely accused of something, being arrested is a somewhat humiliating experience. I was taken in handcuffs in front of my family. I was then taken to the police station where I was searched, fingerprinted, and questioned. I was not presumed innocent.

I am not sure what kind of sick game this is, which is being played at the expense of me and my family's future, but it is morally reprehensible and scrapes at the very bottom of the barrel of my pride. My wife and I have decided to sell the farm and we are moving back to Minneapolis pending my appearance at court for a crime I did not commit. I cannot live in a town where there will always be at least a hint of doubt concerning my integrity.

To all of those individuals who have been supportive and kind, I thank you.

Sincerely,

Franklin Jackson

"Are there usually this number of arrests in town?" Jill asked raising one eyebrow.

"No not really." I said taking a drink of my coffee. "The biggest problem we usually see in the police blotter is litter in the park or some kids vandalizing an abandoned shed."

"So, why do you think this is happening now?" she gave me a cocky look.

I got a sick feeling in the pit of my stomach. Franklyn's arrest made me realize there had still been no arrests or even speculation about the hate crimes.

Chapter 16

If I had a choice that Sunday I would have made an excuse so I didn't have to attend dinner at my parent's house. Jill didn't want to miss it and pointed out that it was likely one of the last days of the year it would be nice enough to eat outside. She would win, and I would reluctantly attend.

While the drama in my family was increasing anything defined as a linguistic exchange was decreasing. Eric and my dad sat silently across the table from one another. The two had reached a point where they did not believe the other would listen. My dad was still angry about Danny being arrested for meth and Eric continuing to spend time with her. Eric was upset my dad felt it was any of his business. It was just easier for them both if they kept all communication on a superficial level. It was as though they had both pushed themselves out of the family.

After the food was on the table and everyone was seated I felt even more uncomfortable. I looked around watching my mom pick at her food, Jill chewing, and Eric cutting his meat in a way I thought was a bit passive aggressive. I sighed to try and be disruptive.

My mom broke the silence "This is very good Don. Is it pork?"

"Lamb," my dad said pushing an oversized helping of potato salad into his mouth. "I got it at Sarah's store."

"It's very good dad," I said. "What do you think Eric?"

"Yes," Eric responded to his plate.

"Hey, mom, did I tell you about Norma?" I said trying to bring some bright spot to the grey meal.

"No." She smiled.

"Norma started her second year of classes in mortuary science at the community college."

"That is some good news." My mom took a drink of wine. "How's she liking it?"

"She loves it. I guess her grades are very good."

Eric looked up at my dad "So, I hear that county law enforcement is getting a grant to help with the drug problems in Ofiara?"

"Yes, that's the rumor." My dad said.

Eric rolled his eyes.

Jason walked from the ally to the back yard with Monet walking right next to him. They were both wearing matching bandanas.

"Jason, hey!" I said loudly.

"How's Jason?" Jill asked reaching out and scratching one of Monet's ears.

"Good, I just wanted to let Sarah know we are completely out of hamburger." Jason sat at the end of the picnic table and picked a piece of meat off the tray in the middle.

"Thank you for the forewarning." I said. "Tomorrow I will have to hear about how upset people are I never order enough meat."

Monet jumped up and grabbed the piece of meat Jason was slowly eating. Once in his jaws he dropped it on the ground and grabbed it again so that he could get a firmer hold.

"God damn it." My dad said. "Can't you get that dog under control?"

"Dad!" I said.

"Don, settle down." Jason said, but that was the wrong thing to say.

My dad was irritated by both the dog and Jason. "You are supposed to be in charge of that dog. He spends the entire day running wild around town and I end up dealing with the consequences."

"OK, I am leaving." Jason got up and walked back to the ally with Monet following him.

Eric got up as well and walked off with no one saying a word.

Chapter 17

In the second week of September the Ofiara Utilities Department decided it needed to take some sort of action on the low water pressure. The utilities manager felt that although the water issue was certainly on an emergency, it would be in the best interest of the town to try and conserve water. Within a week all residents of Ofiara received a small post-card size notice which requested everyone participate in a voluntary water preservation effort. We were asked to water lawns only before 7am and after 9pm. Additionally, it was requested people did not use sprinklers for fun or fill pools.

Of course, like all voluntary acts of preservation there are always a handful of people who choose to ignore the request. Everyone knew who they were though as those abusing their privilege were the ones with the deep green lawns and well fed flowers.

There were also those who went further than they needed to go. Many people started to do things like put a brick or two in the tank of their toilet, not rinsing dishes before they placed them in the dishwasher, and timing how long family members were in the shower. The most impressive of efforts though were a large group of individuals who had a community garden at the park just off the lake. One of the members had used a water pump and pumped water from the lake to the garden.

Spring Hill was by all definitions in the first category of abuse, at least in the opinion of the townspeople. While those in town had to deal with their lawns turning brown and dying, the resort shown a brilliant green from across the lake. The resort's pool was filled, water fountains up and running, and of course their golf course looked perfect.

Also in September the feds had returned to Ofiara. There was an ongoing investigation of Franklin and the chemicals which had been found in his barn. Law enforcement searched for informants and leads. They wanted to find a clue which would lead to the bust of the century. What they found was nothing.

One thing which continued to be overlooked was the issue of the hate crimes. It was sad the feds came to town to look for drugs and not people who were causing so much damage to the lives of others simply in the name of hate. Additionally, with the exception of a few people posting fliers for an anti-racism group forming in town, there was almost no talk about what had happened to the teacher and the farm worker. The thing is homophobia didn't seem all far away from racism. I wondered how long it would be until something was spray painted on my car.

I caught John outside the church the Monday after my dad had snapped at Jason. He was sweeping the front walk and picking up trash.

"Hey you." I smiled.

"Hola," John replied.

I sat down on a marble planter filled with flowers. "I haven't seen you in a while, thought I would stop."

John laughed. "That's usually my job."

"Seriously, what up?"

"I'm just tired."

"Why?" I asked.

"All the crap. It feels like every time I turn around there is another issue." John said sitting down next to me. "Remember Brian Kirkpatrick?"

"Yes." I said. Brian was a few years behind John and I in high school. He was a football player and the guy everyone liked. He was like a younger version of John.

"You know he was deployed to the Middle East."

I nodded.

"I'm not completely sure what happened. Every time his mom starts to talk about it she sobs uncontrollably."

"I had no idea." I said.

"I'm not sure anyone is really thinking about Brian."

I put my head on John's shoulder and he put his arm around me. We both looked up at the same time to see Peter right in front of us. Peter seemed to have the subtly of someone with a broken leg trying to after a dog.

"God bless you Peter." John said very genuinely.

"The sermon on Sunday was great Father John, very inspiring" said Peter. "It's sad you missed it Sarah."

"I'm not much for church Peter."

"It was about how we make water into a symbol for God" said John. "Water is one of those things that make us feel we are near to God."

"Indeed, those who are blessed with the resource must feel especially close to him." said Peter with a big smile. "A blessing like this magnificent lake."

"I guess it depends on how you get the water." John said.

"Are you trying to make a point Father John?" asked Peter.

"You are taking advantage of the situation." John replied.

"What I am doing is economically saving this shit hole from turning into a ghost town." said Peter with an indignant tone in his voice.

"What you are doing, what Polar is doing is nothing more than a short term solution. It will cause more damage to Ofiara than good." said John.

Peter looked at me and asked "What do you think Sarah?"

Just then Jacqueline walked over and joined the conversation. I felt a wave of relief wash over me when I realized I was saved from having to give my opinion. She looked at Peter and sighed.

"Peter, Sarah tries to stay somewhat neutral in situations like we have going on right now. Unfortunately, I don't have that option." John said looking at Peter.

"Let me make something very painfully clear. I am not the bad guy here. John, people like you want the world to be all sunshine, butterflies," Peter then looked directly at me and said "and rainbows. Do you really think that not taking this chance, a chance which could really help your town is somehow honorable? Do you think you are doing a good deed? Do you think the flowers and the lake are going to thank you? No, they aren't." He smiled and sat back a little smugly, "However, when the family down the street is able to send their oldest child to college they will thank me. They will thank me because they have the economic power to send their child to school. They will think of you as just some tree hugger who wanted to save a few drops of water and prevent them from attaining the employment which would help feed their family."

"Wow, you have got it all figured out. Milton Friedman would be so proud wouldn't he." said John.

"Friedman." said Jacqueline half under her breath rolling her eyes.

"I see the apple does not fall far from the tree." Said Peter with an undertone of sarcasm.

"I think I have to get over to my dad's house for dinner." I looked at Peter then back at John. "I'll catch you later."

"I have to go as well. I'm driving to Minneapolis where I will take a private plane to Chicago. I am meeting my wife and coming back in the morning." Peter smiled. "Would God give such blessings to someone who is not actually going to do his will?"

"I guess that old saying is true, the devil does shit in the same place twice," said Jacqueline defiantly.

"I'm not sure I understand what that means Jacqueline." I said in a whisper.

"There is a difference between the will of God and the actions of man." John said

"Or women," Jacqueline added.

"People and progress are much more important than trees," Peter said as he walked off. "I hope you all enjoy the rest of your Sunday."

"Have a safe flight Peter." John said in a frustrated tone.

"Au revoir Peter," yelled Jacqueline then whispered under her breath "you ass hole."

Chapter 18

The last half of September was excruciatingly hot. The water restrictions didn't make cooling off any easier and that made people irritable. People could have cooled down in the lake except it was the time of year that there was a bacteria in the lake called swimmers itch. We could go swimming in the lake but would have to take a shower right after to reduce the chance of getting pock marks all over the body. Most people decided to just not take the chance. Instead, they would sit in their air conditioned homes and out of the warm weather.

Though most town residents didn't talk about the reasons they were pissed, everyone knew. They knew it was the water and their lack of it. Their kids could not run through the sprinkler, instead their kids would sit outside, whining loudly that they had nothing to do and it was too hot.

The utilities department had sent out another notice about the new water restrictions. It had taken only two weeks for the utilities manager to become concerned about the water level in the town wells. The city was no longer restricting times residents watered their lawn; instead people could not water their lawns at all.

What became a sore spot with the town was the fact that water restrictions had not extended to Spring Hill. The resort looked like a heavenly oasis across the lake. It just didn't feel fair.

On the home front, Jill was being somewhat secretive with me. This made me extremely curious. She was spending a great deal of time with my brother and his friends. The secrecy going on with my partner, friends, and my brother would be the backdrop for a protest for which I would become an unwilling participant.

It was a hot lazy Sunday night; by all accounts perfect. There was no wind to speak of and Jill talked me into an evening drive. We drove around the back roads for a bit and finally ended up at the road which entered Spring Hill.

"What are we doing?" I asked Jill a little bit nervous. Spring Hill was well out of my comfort zone. It was that place above me, clean and polished perfect people.

"I think it's a nice night for hanging out at the pool." She said grinning.

Just as she said that a second set of headlights came up from behind.

"Oh God." I said with increasing fear. I knew there was something wrong even though I could not voice it. It is that same feeling as walking through a dark neighborhood at night. I wasn't aware what the danger was I felt, but I knew damn well it was there.

When the headlights behind us turned off I realized it was Eric's truck.

"Damn it!" I muttered to myself. I knew I had full freedom at that point. I could have walked back to town or just taken the car.

I got out of the car and walked back seeing not just Eric. He had also brought Jake and Todd.

"Are we going to do this?" Jake asked with his typically cocky attitude. He was taking a drink out of an energy drink he had purchased at the grocery store earlier, a drink created and produced by Polar Beverage.

"What exactly are you guys doing?" I asked.

"Let's go." said Jill.

Jill walked back up to the car and I got into the passenger seat.

I looked at Jill and demanded "I really have to know what the hell we are doing?"

"Sarah, it's no longer optional to not take a side." Jill said.

The thing is, Jill may have been right. I knew things were changing. However, despite the certainties of Jill and a handful of others I did not feel the same imperative feelings. The only certainty I had was that I disliked being forced to make a decision on limited information.

Eric drove around us and Jill then followed his truck. Both vehicles had headlights off as they drove slowly up the road to the resort then down a hill next to the golf course. At the edge of the course was an inviting kidney shaped pool.

Everyone got out of their vehicles. I walked next to the pool feeling the pungent smell of chlorine in my nose. I stood on the edge ready to jump in when Eric backed up his old truck. It was filled with what looked like extra large sand or flour bags. The foursome quickly and nervously pulled bags from the back of the truck. They opened the bags with knives and box cutters then emptied a white powdery substance into the pool.

It took me several minutes to realize what was happening. Finally, I realized the powder would gel up and clump in whatever area it was dumped. It looked as if the pool was filling with an almost transparent substance with the consistency of cottage cheese.

This went on for several bags until I started to take an active role in the vandalism. I just wanted to get the hell out of their and it seemed as though that wouldn't happen until the bags were emptied. I will admit, there was a part of me that was starting to feel a bit of a rush at doing something very illegal.

When we finished our work we all took one quick look. Eric placed a lawn chair on the top of the gelled up gunk which now filled the pool. The chair just sat there without sinking to the bottom.

The guys drove off in Eric's truck and Jill and I started walking towards the car. I felt shaky.

"Oh, fuck me," whispered Jill as she grabbed me and pulled me to the ground.

"What the hell are you doing?" I asked.

"Be quiet." She said smiling. "Look, there." She pointed towards a group of town houses that looked over the pool and the golf course.

An extremely built and handsome man was slowly leaving one of the townhouses. He appeared to be saying good night to his lover or at the very least a brief passionate encounter with another man. The younger man looked over and gave a whimsical look and blew a kiss to Peter who grinned.

"He's such an ass hole." Jill whispered.

When we got back to the house Jill grabbed me from behind, turned me around, and kissed me.

"That was exhilarating," she said. "Have you ever felt so good about something?"

"Jill, I don't feel comfortable with what we just did." I replied taking off my shoes.

"We did something awesome tonight, we took a stand."

I was visibly irritated "Really, because I missed that part. What exactly did we take a stand against?"

"Tonight we told Polar Beverage we know what they are doing and we don't like it." said Jill trying to convince me our efforts and the damage we had inflicted had meant something.

"I didn't see us telling anyone anything. What we did tonight is create a big mess resort maintenance is going to have to clean up. A couple of guys who make barely more than the minimum wage will spend hours fixing our mess. Most likely, Peter is never going to see what happened and if he does he will just walk past. All we've done is to make life more difficult for the people who already have a difficult life."

"You think this was for nothing?" Jill loudly responded.

I looked down at the ground to avoid her stare. "You do this; you take any information and turn it into a truth or a fact and feel that you know better than anyone else. Then, as though you feel you have the market cornered on morality you make a statement declaring your assumptions. You're not the person who gets to decide what is right for all the people in this world or in this town."

"Do you really think we are that far removed from a little village in India? Do you truly feel something like that doesn't in some way touch us? The world is all interconnected. Everything we do touches others just like the actions of a few bad managers at Polar damages the world. We bought these products and supported this corporation and integrated it into what we called the American Dream. And, now what they have done warp the American Dream is in this town. We are no longer that removed from a little village in India."

"You have missed the entire point Jill. You dragged me into something, without me understanding or knowing what was going on. Did you stop to think that this was not my fight or did you just assume I would support this because you are telling me what is right and wrong? Did you think at all?"

"Isn't that what Polar Beverage, you, and your dad are doing by not telling people what they have a history of doing?"

I sighed. "I am going to bed now." I walked upstairs.

Jill didn't come to bed that night. I'm not sure she slept at all. We both drew a line in the sand that night, indicating to the other our limits.

Chapter 19

Two days later, on a hazy Tuesday afternoon, Todd was arrested for the pool incident. The white powder we had put into the pool was a chemical used by the paper company in Grand Rapids where both Todd and Jake worked. Methylcellulose, as it's called, is used to create specialty papers. It also happened to be the same chemical that Todd was in charge of using at the plant. It was Todd who was now facing jail time, in addition to losing his job at the plant. If the humiliation of being arrested was not enough, the arresting officer was Terry.

Sitting in court the following Wednesday, I thought about how things in Ofiara seemed to keep going downhill. Until Polar Beverage had moved into town I had never been to court for any reason. Suddenly, in the last few months I had been there with friends several times. It was getting to be tiring and demoralizing.

The longer I sat in that courtroom, the angrier I became at Jill. She had blindly pulled me into a fight I didn't understand or really agree with. The worst part was that Jill didn't even try to apologize for what happened. How could I forgive someone who had no remorse?

Todd was lucky enough to get Janet Mason. She was able to get the judge to set his bail at ten thousand dollars. That was money he didn't have to just throw around, but he had no other choice than to pay it. Though nothing was said, my gut feeling was there was much more evidence against Todd than there had been against Danny.

Jill was still at work when I got home from court, which, to be perfectly honest, was a relief. The house was quiet and free from stress. Douglas walked over a few minutes after I got through the door. We went down to the dock and sat at the end.

Douglas had a bottle of Greek Ouzo and two crystal lowball glasses. I poured a drink and placed my feet in the water while taking my first sip "Yum."

After his third refill, Douglas started to talk about what had happened. "Today, I witnessed ignorance," he said as he took another drink.

"Was it blissful?"

"Nope, can't say it was."

"Oh, that sucks," I said with a sigh with the smell of the clear liquor filling my nose.

"Part of Polar Beverage's mission is to hire minorities, not because it is the right thing to do, but because it conveys to the rest of the world that we are doing the right thing. We hired this guy, Matt, to work in human resources. Nice guy and years of experience in both accounting and HR. Then, today, right before this guy is supposed to start, Peter gets up in front of the entire crew and announces that they finally hired an HR person, but that the hiring of this person was going to cost the plant. He told the crew that the plant would have to be made wheelchair accessible."

"Charming," I said, taking a drink. "Was the guy Matt Bergen?" I asked.

"Yes," Douglas responded with a sigh at the end.

"I used to work with Matt," I stated. "He's smart. Not sure why he would want to work at Polar."

"Hey, the money is good."

"What do you mean it was going to cost the plant?" I asked realizing the Ouzo may have caused me to miss a bit of what Douglas was trying to say.

"He told them, quite clearly, that they had to make changes to the plant, reasonable accommodations. He then went on to tell the crew that because there was such a high cost for these accommodations, we won't be able to hire additional workers."

"Wow," I said, taking a big gulp.

"Can you imagine how this guy is going to be treated by his coworkers? He's going to be ostracized, treated like the building villain."

"What are you going to do?" I asked.

"Well, a small part of me is hoping I will get a touch of alcohol poisoning and have to be rushed to Grand Rapids. Ideally, I would like to be in intensive care long enough to avoid the next few weeks."

"Douglas, you are going to have to do better than that if your goal is to end up in a coma."

"Oh, thanks," he said sarcastically and we both laughed.

"Do you know why Matt is in a wheelchair?" I asked Douglas.

"No, we are not actually allowed to ask that," Douglas responded. "Is it important to know?"

"I'm not sure." I paused and said, "Douglas, with all due respect I think you are underestimating the workers at the plant. This may turn out better than you think."

"Well, I hope you're right. Half of every one of my workdays is consumed by the dueling idiots who have been given the positions of shift managers. It's like a pissing contest that just goes on and on. They complain and complain." Douglas said and finished off the remainder of the clear liquid in his glass.

"Hey, when is your girlfriend moving up?" I said trying to change the subject.

Douglas gave me a sour look. "No idea."

Chapter 20

With the onset of October, Ofiara cooled down and the water restrictions became an afterthought. Granted, there was still the same issue with the water pressure, but it didn't seem as significant as when it was hot. Most people didn't water their lawns in the fall or send their kids through the sprinklers in the cold air.

The roads were covered with a thick coat of multi-colored leaves as Jill and I drove to Eric's house for chili. The two of us were just inches apart in the car, but I felt so detached. It was like I was in a bubble and she was outside. No matter how much I loved her, I found myself fighting the feeling that I was in the car with a stranger. I felt like we were living out some cheesy '80's song.

Jill had been even more secretive with me since the pool incident. I had a feeling something else was going to happen, something bad. I just wasn't sure what that would be. Jill and Danny had been spending a great deal of time together, which made me more than a little jealous. It wasn't that I thought there was something going on between Danny and Jill. I was jealous over Danny getting to see a side of Jill she no longer shared with me. Danny got to see the passionate side of Jill.

No one was at the main house so we had to walk back to the cabin. There was a strong cold mist coupled with the wind coming off the lake. I looked behind me making sure Jill was still there. She was like a hooded ghost, not completely there.

When we finally reached the cabin Eric and Danny were sitting close together on the couch, with Danny's hand on Eric's knee. She moved it abruptly as we walked in.

"Hola!" said Jill.

"Hey there," said Danny.

"Did you see Todd and Jake on the way in?"

"Nope," I answered.

The entire cabin smelled like the pot of chili that was on the stove.

"Oh, that smells so good," Jill said.

"I agree," replied Danny. "Eric has been working on it all morning."

Eric stood up and walked towards the refrigerator, stopping at the table. He grabbed a pile of about four white t-shirts and brought them to the bedroom. Without missing a beat, he was back and grabbed two beers handing one to me then Jill.

"Hey, you are starting to pick up after yourself. A sign of progress." I said, opening my beer.

The door opened and John walked in with a box filled with rope and duct tape. John looked away.

"Hi Sarah," said John, without telling me what the items in the box were for.

Anger started to bubble up inside me. There was something going on that I didn't know about.

I looked over at Eric. "Are you and Danny going over to Dad's tomorrow for dinner?"

"I can't," Eric answered. "I have a lot of stuff going on, and then I also have to study safety codes and the employee handbook for Polar."

"Eric, it won't take that long to study and I am sure Dad would really like to see you," I said, trying to get him to reconsider.

Eric looked at me with a sober resolution. "No Sarah. Please drop it."

"OK. I won't push it," I said, looking at the floor.

"Thank you," he replied.

Just then Todd and Jake entered the cabin, each of them carrying a mannequin. It looked as though there were two more outside.

"Hello gentleman, ladies, and..." Jake said and then looked at Jill and me, finishing with, "...lesbians."

"What the hell is going on?" I asked, feeling a little left out of whatever they were doing.

"A guy has needs," responded Todd. "There are some things not even Jake can do for me."

"Where did you get them?" I asked.

"My mom, she got them free when some department store in Duluth closed down. Remember when she used to make all of my clothes?"

"Oh yeah, that was kind of sad, John," I said "So, why are her sewing buddies being pulled out of storage now?"

No one said anything. Instead, they looked either uncomfortably at me or down at the floor.

"You know what, that's fine. If you don't want to tell me that's just fine," I said, irritated now.

"I am sorry, we're perverts," said Jake apologetically.

Eric started to get very defensive. "Sarah, you don't seem to want to engage in any activity that would question the high and mighty Polar Beverage, so it is difficult to include you."

"You know what, I don't want to know." It would have been hard to miss how much my feelings had been hurt. "What I think is that all of you are going a bit overboard. The doors on the plant have hardly opened. You are all jumping to conclusions and acting out in a way that is nothing more than juvenile."

"Sis," said Eric.

"Yeah, and you know what Eric?" I said, my voice getting louder. "Polar is good enough for you to accept a pay check from." I pointed at him. "You're a fucking hypocrite."

Danny cut in. "We are going to have some chili. Do you want some?"

"Fuck you," I said, grabbing my jacket and putting it on.

Jill attempted to grab my arm, but I pulled away from her harshly.

I decided to drive back to town. It was clear no one was going to share what they were doing. They either did not trust me or did not want to hear disagreement with what they were doing. In either case, it seemed best to remove myself from the situation.

Chapter 21

Two days following my outburst at the cabin, on a sunny Monday morning, Norma and her two children were walking past the plant to get to work. As she walked past Polar Beverage the bottling plant's day shift was arriving for work. A group mainly made up of males was standing at the front entrance. The workers were looking at three mannequins tied to the fence with rope. The figures had been set up in "see no evil, hear no evil, and speak no evil" poses. All three plastic women wore t-shirts with sayings such as, "Polar Beverage sucks." Two of the workers, one of them being Sam, cut the dolls from their rope and then made sexual gestures with the inanimate females. They put their hands over the women's breasts and pretended to penetrate the unwilling plastic females from behind.

"This is not ok," Norma said after finishing her story. Her face got close to mine and she whispered "assholes," so her kids couldn't hear it.

"I agree," I said, feeling the embarrassment from knowing who was behind the stunt.

Norma's daughters sat at a card table next to the window playing a game of Candy Land. She sometimes brought them into the store while she worked. They seemed to like it and she felt better about all the hours school and work seemed to take away from them.

"Who the heck do all these people think they are?" she said, grabbing a cleaning cloth from the closet. She started wiping down the counter and then moved to the front window.

"It was just wrong," I said.

"I heard a rumor from Dean," Norma said, not removing her eyes from her work.

"Dean spreads a lot of rumors; that is the problem with being retired. He has too much time on his hands," I said

Norma laughed. "Dean said that he had heard the utilities department was thinking about raising water prices."

"Really?"

"Well, that is what he said."

"I haven't heard anything," I replied.

"Your dad hasn't said anything?" Norma replied, probing further.

"No, that is something I would have remembered."

"If you do hear something let me know. Money is already so tight for me, Sarah." She smiled back at me "My budget is down to the penny."

"Yes ma'am, I will tell you if I hear anything."

Douglas walked through the front door and headed for the produce section with a small wave of acknowledgement to me.

"Hey," I said loudly. "I hear there was a little chaos going on at the plant this morning."

"Yeah," Douglas made his way up to the counter with a bag of apples. "The plant wasn't the only place it happened. Your friends decided to send a message to me as well." I could tell he was angry.

"My friends?" I replied.

"When I walked out my front door today, there was a mannequin bent over my car wearing only a t-shirt that read, "Grow a pair and do something.""

"Oh my God, Douglas, I am so sorry," I said. "I didn't have anything to do with this."

"I know, and I get what they are trying to say, but that was such a shitty way to try and get a message across."

"I think they were trying to be shocking, trying to get people's attention."

"Well, they got Peter's attention. He was shaken up and now he is just angry." Doulas looked down. "They need to think a little more about the messages they decide to put out there."

Later that day, John called and apologized. He was the only one out of the six conspirators to admit what happened, let alone feel some sort of regret about what they had done. He said he really didn't think things were going to go that far. He seemed to be the only one with a sense of humility.

Chapter 22

The beginning of November, we finally received news about Danny's trial. In fact, there would not be one. The case was dropped. Janice spent a few months exchanging emails with the county attorneys. She had let them know they didn't have a case and that she would be more than willing to let the trial go on for months, costing the state thousands. The county came to know Janice was serious; they also found out she had a very high win rate.

The case being dropped didn't mean people would forgive or forget the fact Danny had been arrested. The damage was done. People continued to associate Danny with meth. Most felt it wasn't a case of being innocent as much as it was a case of law enforcement not finding enough evidence. In our small town, human weakness, context, and of course motives did not matter. Someone committing such a crime was symbolically lynched. Even if that person was later shown to be innocent, such as in the case of Danny. People in town would say things like, "Well, if she hadn't been running with drug dealers, it wouldn't have happened in the first place" or "That is sometimes the price of keeping our town drug-free." It was like fear of humility, the humility to admit they were wrong.

Chapter 23

Somewhere in the course of the tenth night of November, the first few flakes of snow hit the streets of Ofiara. Of course, this act of nature led almost everyone in town to speculate about the kind of a winter it was going to be. My dad felt it was going to be a harsh winter. I had to agree with my dad, I could feel it.

The morning after that first snow, I arrived at the store to be greeted with the word "Dyke" spray painted on the store's front window. The paint was green, my favorite color, but I doubt the perpetrator knew that. I flushed red as I realized I was a victim. There was someone in town that either didn't like me or was not comfortable with my presence.

I went into the store and grabbed some steel wool and cleaning solvents. Honestly, I didn't care how badly I scratched the glass, I just wanted it gone. I had flashbacks to those days in the closet and just wanted to go back in, to take it all back, and to be hidden from the world. In my heart I knew the word was nothing more than an attempt to put me in my place. A bully on the playground meticulously making sure that his or her victims remained docile and silent. That's how the game is played. Regardless of this knowledge, I didn't feel any better about it. I wanted to be back into a place where I didn't have to feel so self-conscious.

I called Terry. Her deputy car was parked down the street in front of the Catholic Church. I disliked having to ask her for help almost as much the paint I was trying to remove from the glass on my storefront. Unfortunately, I just didn't have a choice, and some help was possibly better than none.

Dean walked up from behind and looked at the image on the door. It seemed for a moment as though he was trying to understand the word. "White trash homophobic assholes."

"I am so embarrassed," I said, looking down.

Dean put his hand on my shoulder. "Sarah my dear, you are better than this. I'll get the cash register set up." He then walked inside the store.

"Dean, you're not scheduled," I said.

Dean rolled his eyes and then walked inside to get things set up for the day.

I turned around and saw Douglas.

"I was walking to work and I saw." He grabbed a rag out of the bucket and started scrubbing on the "K".

"This is really stupid."

"Oh Sarah," he said with a sigh.

Douglas continued to scrub until the second half of the spray painted image was gone.

"I've got to get running to work." Douglas smiled. throwing his rag in the bucket.

"Thank you Douglas," I said with a half smile.

Terry finally showed up two hours later and I described what had happened.

"That is awful, Sarah," she said. "Can you show me?"

"I cleaned it off," I replied.

"Did you get pictures?" she asked.

"No, I just wanted it off the window." A feeling of helplessness washed over me. Perhaps the same feeling the mannequins would have felt if they had been alive.

"Sarah, I cannot do anything without any evidence."

"You're kidding!"

"I wish I could." Terry said putting away a small notebook she was holding.

That was the exact point where I snapped. The part of me which had been trying to ride the fence line for so long was gone. "No you don't!"

"Excuse me?" Terry said, on the defensive.

I pointed at the door where the word had been written. "Some village idiots do this, and you can't do anything about it?"

A few people had started to filter into the store. They walked past, staring at the vocal showdown between me and the deputy. Two of the audience members were Ester and her younger sister Bonnie. The two women stopped and watched the exchange between Terry and me.

"I am tired of this."

"Tired of what exactly?" she asked.

"I am tired of seeing you try and pass off what you do as a deputy as your job. And, by the way, I called you hours ago and you just showed up," I said in an exhausted tone.

"I was down the street on business."

"What, were you at confession down there with Father John? You had better schedule an entire afternoon for that!" My tone was slowly but surely elevating.

I realized that one went a bit far. It was like an out of body experience or watching myself on TV. Somewhere, in the back of my head, there was a part of myself cheering, telling me to go further and further.

"You know what? You are the same bitch now that you were in high school. You always felt you were better than everyone else because you got a fucking scholarship!" she yelled back.

"Fuck you, Terry!"

"Go to hell, Sarah!"

Terry walked out of the store slowly. As soon as she was out the door I felt a little bad about the things I had said. Not completely bad. It wasn't that I felt any less dislike for Terry; it was just that I was taking out my frustrations on her.

I took a seat behind the counter next to the cash register. I knew it was coming. Ester would have to say something. Usually, it was some sort of complaint about the produce prices or quality. When I explained to her, on many occasions, a grocery store in Ofiara Minnesota is not competitive with a large supermarket, she never seemed to understand. Quite simply, our prices could never be as low as those in one of the grocery stores in Grand Rapids, because we can't order in large quantities.

Ester was what most people would define as an egocentric. She had the type of mindset which was reflective of a two year old. She was completely unable to see past herself. It could very well have been she didn't think anyone in town shopped at that little grocery store, other than her and her sister. Ester was a former Water Carnival queen, who married right out of high school. Twenty years her senior, he owned the biggest car dealership in the area. She asked him to buy her the biggest home in Ofiara. He purchased a grand three story Victorian, which overlooked the lake. It had 8 bedrooms and 3 bathrooms. She had it made. In fact, her husband gave her everything she wanted, at least until he found a younger model. When Ester was forty years old, her husband announced he was leaving her for a younger woman, nineteen years younger than Ester.

Ester brought one banana and a bag of rice to the counter. She slowly placed her items on the counter without looking at me, waiting for me to ring her things up. Her body looked so frail, as though even a light breeze would make her skin flap like a flag in the wind.

"Hi Ester," I said with an exhausted smile. She said nothing as she watched me ring up her groceries. "That will be three dollars and forty three cents."

"A little expensive, don't you think?" she replied, looking at me as though I was going to run over to the aisle and start slashing prices immediately.

"Well, the banana is the same price it always is, but you bought a much larger bag of rice than usual."

"Oh, so I did." Instead of acknowledging her mistake Ester took an accusatory tone towards me, as if it were somehow my fault.

"Would you like a bag for that?"

"Yes, yes, please. You know, such a scene is not good for business." she stated with her eyes lowered to her purse, fumbling around and counting out her money, making sure to get rid of all of her pennies.

"What sort of scene?" I asked.

"Well, when I came in I heard there was a bad word painted on the door. Someone had painted a homosexual word," she said, as she continued to rummage for change. Now she was on to nickels. She got frustrated when she realized didn't have enough coins. She opened the bill area of her wallet and pulled out fifty dollars.

"Yes, but it really wasn't something I had anything do to with," I replied, anticipating the conversational car accident just about to happen.

"Dear," she said, looking up at me with a condescending look, as if I could not understand what she was trying to say. "It was your choice to live your lifestyle, the one God does not want."

"I'm sorry Ester, are you saying I got what I deserved?"

"What I am saying is that it is not up to you to question God's word. I thought you were brought up in a good home. I guess I just don't understand."

I just stood there internally trying to detach myself, so as to not tell off the elderly lady in the store. Just then, I was saved by Bonnie balancing several pounds of ground beef, noodles, and sour cream in her arms.

"Sarah, help?" she smiled.

"Yes," I said quickly, walking around the corner and grabbing items from the top of the giant pile she was carrying.

Bonnie was a positive to all of Ester's negatives. She was always smiling and volunteering for local charities. She was a person who made the lives of those around her better.

Ester walked towards the door. She reminded me of Nosferatu looking for a new victim. She then looked back finding her target. "You need to stop feeding that damn dog, Sarah. You feed something to that mutt, and it will never leave."

"I'll keep that in mind," I said, turning to look at Bonnie, who was smiling sympathetically.

"I wanted to tell you, I met Jill while walking past your house the other night with Tom," she said, pulling out her check book.

"Yeah?" I said with a smile, not really knowing what to expect, but reaching for a scrap of optimism.

"She seems very lovely."

It was only a few words, but that short exchange had made me feel quite a bit better.

When I left work that afternoon I noticed Eric's car parked outside Jacqueline's house. This didn't surprise me. They now shared a common goal, and really, no group of people is more united than a group of people which has come together over a common enemy.

Chapter 24

December had been the coldest on record in the town of Ofiara. Most days that month it rarely got above minus five Fahrenheit. This created an added obstacle for the residents who lived in the trailer park on the edge of town who had to crawl under their homes with heating tape, wrapping it around their water pipes. If they didn't do this, the water in the pipes would freeze and eventually burst.

Mid-month marked the formal closing of the ventilation plant. Absent anything which resembled a formal ceremony, the doors were sealed shut and the last few employees went home. Another piece of the Ofiara's history was gone and would soon be forgotten.

Most of those who worked at In-House had been able to attain jobs at Polar. Sadly, there were a handful of men and women who were not quite that lucky. These individuals were able to apply for unemployment, but faced a grim assignment. The task which they had been unwillingly given was to find employment in the economically downtrodden iron range of northern Minnesota. Additionally, they had to look for jobs during the winter when jobs were most scarce.

Peter's image quickly moved from businessman to superhero with one act of charity. On the last day of school before Christmas break, he walked into the educational administration offices with a check for twenty five thousand dollars. Teachers, parents, and students were more than ecstatic about the donation. The money meant the school could buy the computers needed to graduate students who would stand more of a chance in a post-secondary environment. What they didn't realize was that the donation was part of Polar's deal with the town. It wasn't an altruistic act of kindness, but rather a business transaction. Additionally, it was much less than the fifty thousand he had promised.

The timing of Peter's alleged grand act of generosity became apparent a few days later at the city council meeting. He addressed the council and stated Polar would need to drill another well in the spring. He then explained that building a new well was critical to the future of the plant and without it; Polar Beverage would have to reconsider its ability to continue to operate in Ofiara. It looked like the ugly face of extortion coated with sugar.

Jacqueline and her entourage had failed to make an appearance at that particular December city council meeting. It bothered me that they had made such a stink about how much damage Polar would cause and then just dropped the subject.

A final item which was added to the city council agenda was the household water issue. The utilities department had very successfully decreased water usage with the lawn watering restrictions. Although this had been the perfect short-term solution, the water pressure and noises coming from the pipes didn't appear to be getting any better; in fact, they were getting significantly worse. Normally, in the fall and throughout the winter, water consumption per household went significantly lower than the summer months. Unfortunately, that year was different, and water consumption increased.

The head of the municipal water and electric plant was Scotty Thomson. He was a short man with a large growth above his eye, not the greatest to look at. However, this vertically challenged man had come up with an idea which he felt would significantly decrease the water difficulties. During the meeting, Scotty asserted residents of Ofiara were good and hard working people, but perhaps would not voluntarily submit to water restrictions. His solution was to increase the price of water. The current price was three cents a gallon; the proposed new price was going to be nine cents a gallon. Everyone on the city council felt this was a brilliant decision and decided that it was what they would do.

Just before Christmas, Danny and Eric came over for dinner. Eric talked almost nonstop about growing tensions within the plant. There had been a great deal of arguing and bickering. Eric talked about the trouble between Juan and Sam. Both men had procured their own small groups of followers, mainly in the shifts they supervised. Sam would tell people that when Juan was working things would not be done or cleaned for the following shift. Juan's shift had the highest production of any of the shifts and would say Sam was simply jealous because his crew moved so slowly. It went on and on. The bickering of the two angry men was eating away at the workers at the plant.

It wasn't just strained relationships between the shift leaders. Someone decided to pull the wheelchair ramp away from the front doors of Polar. When the ramp was first installed, it was angled in a way which almost created a blind spot. A person leaving the building in a chair wasn't going to see whether or not the ramp was there. Although this posed some trust issues, it didn't enter people's minds as even a possibility that someone would remove the ramp.

Matt Bergen, the human resources director was leaving the evening before Christmas Eve. Making his way out to his van, he ended up pushing himself off the five feet high edge. Fortunately, the snow broke his fall and several people quickly came to his aid.

Chapter 25

Peter flew home to Chicago on Christmas Eve, leaving Douglas in charge of the plant. Before he left he gave everyone the night off and a vacation day for Christmas. Douglas seemed quite happy to see Peter gone for a few days.

Jill decided to invite people over for Christmas Eve. My family, extended family, and friends showed up early and started to drink and eat as soon as they arrived. Jill had even invited Terry, which irritated me. I didn't want Terry even driving past the house, let alone inside, eating my food or sitting on my furniture.

A few hours into things, Eric, Danny, Jake, and Todd all disappeared. I had assumed they were smoking pot. It was around the same time Jill cornered Terry at the party. I have no idea what they were talking about and didn't have quite enough energy to care. Initially, Terry seemed a bit irritated with Jill, until she saw Jill hanging on her every word, and then she started to eat it up.

I walked over and asked Terry, "You're not going to Midnight Mass?"

"Well, hello, Sarah. I've hardly seen you all night." Terry responded.

"You know, John will be there," I said with a half grin. "They need a priest to preside over services."

"Dear," Jill rubbed my shoulder. "Could you set out some more cheese and crackers?"

"It'll go well with your wine," Terry said, looking at Jill and avoiding eye contact with me.

I walked into the kitchen where Jacqueline was sitting with Jason and Douglas, telling stories about working in the South and other activist activities. Douglas countered her stories with the things he had done while working with an environmentalist movement in Africa and South America. For quite a while they took turns exchanging knowledge and ideas. Unfortunately, Jacqueline seemed to drive the conversation back to Polar again and again. Throughout the conversation I caught Douglas looking at me with wide eyes, silently pleading for help.

Surprisingly, due to the cold weather, my dad invited Monet into the house. Granted, what he felt free to do at my house he was unlikely to do at his. However, it's always easier to volunteer the resources of another person. The canine sat watching the conversation at the table. I threw a few pieces of sausage over to him which made him jump. He then looked back at me and tilted his head as though to say, "Thank you." Monet could also have been begging, but who really knows.

After a while Danny or Jake started to wander in and out of the kitchen and talk to whoever was there, very nonchalantly. One would grab some cheese and yet another would grab a bottle of wine. It looked as though they were having their own separate party someplace in the house, which more than irritated me. Finally, it occurred to me they were again up to something, and I again didn't know what.

A half hour into Jill's conversation with Terry, I looked out the back window to see Jake walking over to Eric's truck and placing something under the driver's seat. He looked up at me with a mischievous grin and placed a finger over his mouth to signal me to keep quiet. Over the next few minutes, the four members of this group integrated back into the party, eating, laughing, and of course drinking. I knew my short moment of peace was over.

When I woke up Christmas morning I went downstairs to make coffee. With the beverage plant shut down for Christmas I was pleasantly surprised to find the water pressure almost normal. After I finished my coffee it also occurred to me I could take a shower, so I did that as well. After a few phone calls, I found out the water pressure was much better throughout the entire town.

Chapter 26

It was a bitterly cold Christmas night. We only had to walk a few blocks to my dad's house for dinner, although it felt like miles. Jill and I were wearing snowsuits, scarves, and thick mittens. The world was still and quiet, making our footsteps loud and crunchy against the snow.

"So, what happened last night?" I asked, watching as my words formed a cloud floating out of my mouth.

"What do you mean?" she asked innocently.

"I am talking about all the disappearing and reappearing. Does any of that ring a bell?"

Jill laughed and said, "No idea what you mean."

"What were you guys doing?" I asked a little irritated.

"You may not be aware of this, but you are also morally flawed, Sarah. You sit there, analyzing everything but you never do anything. You place every action onto some sort of abstract sliding scale of right and wrong. The problem is you're the person who decides the terms of this sliding scale and no one else gets any sort of say."

"OK, I have no idea what you did, but I'm reaching my breaking point. It's cold, we better go," I responded, feeling the indignity bubbling to the surface. For a moment, I couldn't move and just watched as Jill made her way through the snow. I was angry, frustrated, and most of all, tired.

Later that evening, after John had made all of his Christmas rounds, visiting those who were alone, sick, or dying, he made it to my dad's house for some company and leftovers from dinner. I sat with him as he picked through the gluttony of what was Christmas dinner.

"So," I smiled. "Merry Christmas."

John smiled back at me, "Yes," he said, as he took a bite of an olive. "It was nice to see everyone enjoying the holiday."

"Please tell me you had nothing to do with what happened last night," I said.

"Nope, actually I didn't," John said.

"Did you know about it?" I asked, almost afraid of the answer.

"Sarah, please."

I sighed and said, "OK."

I paused and decided to dive into an even more dangerous area. "You and Terry have been spending a great deal of time together."

"Terry has been stopping by a lot, yep," he said very bluntly, looking me straight in the eyes. I looked down in discomfort.

"Well then, what is going on?" I asked. "Confession?"

"No," John said. "But if it was, I couldn't tell you." John smelled the potatoes and took a bite. "Anyway, she was just fishing."

"For what?" I asked.

"I'm not sure, but I know fishing when I see it."

"I know I am being a nag. I just want to make sure you are doing ok."

"Remember when that farmer had the thing about the KKK written on his truck?"

"Yes."

"A few days later I saw the truck drive through town. I thought there was something strange in the writing."

"And?" I asked.

"I walked over to my mom's house and looked at some of my old high school notes she had saved for me." John grinned, "You know the kind of thing she wanted to save for me in case I left the priesthood."

"Oh yes, I remember the box." I smiled.

"I wanted to look at the letter T in the notes. Terry had this strange way of crossing the T at the beginning of her name." John put his finger in the air and drew a curve. "It was like a wave."

"Was it the same T that was on the truck?"

"It was lower-case, but the curve of the line was the same," John said, pushing his food around the plate a little. "Sarah, it really could just be a coincidence."

"Yeah."

"There is one more thing."

"What?" I asked.

"The meth bust, that Franklyn Jackson? Do you know whose old farmhouse he bought?"

"Nope," I said.

"That was Terry's parents' old farm. That barn, that barn is where I lost my virginity." John grinned and shoved a large piece of turkey in his mouth.

"Very glad you told me that," I said, squinting as if the physical movement would help keep the image out of my head.

"Anyway, that barn was already filled with chemicals, several of the same ones listed in the paper.

"You're not keeping this information on the down-low because you still have this desire to protect Terry? Are you?"

John gave me the stink eye, "Sarah, you are acting stupid. I did call Terry's boss and tell him, but he didn't say if he was going to do anything about it."

"No one is going to do anything." I poured a glass of wine.

"I don't know Sarah," he said.

"And this has nothing to do with leftover feelings for her? Or, feelings she might have for you?"

"Thanks Sarah, that's nice."

"I didn't mean it that way." I took a drink of wine. "And, you would have asked the same question if the situations were reversed."

"You know, I'm still a man, and I'm fallible."

"Yes, I am aware of that John," I paused and then it hit me. "Did she try to sleep with you?"

"Nothing happened. I took my vows, Sarah. I'm not going to break my vows for some lost memory of the past."

"She is just going to get away with this, isn't she?" I asked, rolling my eyes.

"Sarah, you want to know the one thing that sitting in a confessional booth for a few years has taught me?"

"What Father John?" I asked in a formal tone and smiled.

"It has taught me that those people, the ones who do bad things, they do those bad things for a reason. People," he said with a smile, "most people, don't want to do these things, they just don't know another way."

"And we're back to protecting her," I said with defeat in my voice.

"No." John said assertively. "I'm just trying to explain."

"OK John, with all due respect, that does not fly with me. Once Terry turned 18 years old she pretty much became responsible for everything she does."

"But, who we are as people is contingent on everything we have become. All of our memories, hopes, fears, intelligence, and, of course, those bad things we keep inside. We keep all that has been good and bad, someplace, locked up inside of ourselves. And yes, it's our choice what we do with that information, but sometimes we have a self-limited view of what that choice is."

I had started to feel a bit exasperated with the argument. "John, you are trying to validate actions that are, at the very least, cruel. Maybe part of the reason Terry has done these things, including what she did to Danny, is because she has never been held accountable for her actions."

John poured himself a glass of wine. "I understand that Terry needs to be held accountable for her actions."

"OK, that's what I was trying to say," I said, exasperated.

"What she did, if she did it, has broad consequences. No matter what we do, there is a good chance nothing will happen. If she receives no reprimand then everything she has done will come back at us as well as the town, and this time it will be far worse."

"We have to do something." I responded.

Chapter 27

On the fifth of January, residents of Ofiara received their utility bills, only to discover what they were paying for water had now been tripled. This meant that the water bill for some families was close to one hundred and twenty dollars a month for water. Residents were shocked and a little pissed.

On the sixth of January, early in the morning, Ester marched over to my parents' house in the frigid January weather. I could hear footsteps crunching in the snow that morning as I was pulling ice fishing rods out of my parents' garage. I was quiet and still as I watched her walk up the path and knock on the door. It was like watching a villain from an old black and white movie.

My dad answered the door in his blue housecoat, with a cup of coffee in his hand.

"Good morning Ester."

"What is this Mr. Mayor?" she asked, shoving the bill in my dad's face.

"I believe it's your utilities bill," he replied. He didn't mean to sound sarcastic, but it came out that way.

"I understand that, what have you done to the water?" she asked in that tone which placed all of the blame directly on my dad's shoulders.

"I haven't done anything. Ester, this is sometimes just the way things happen," my dad said, trying to be democratic about things.

"Well, this is the first time there has been an increase like this." Ester said shaking the bill back and forth in front of my dad's face.

"I guess so," my dad said, looking tired.

"You were just going to do this and not tell anyone." She replied.

"We did it at the city council meeting, nothing was hidden." My dad shrugged a little.

"I was there, I didn't hear anything." She was getting angrier and angrier at my dad as he tried to explain his reasons to her.

"That is because you didn't stay for the entire meeting. You came in, complained about things such as your issue with the dogs in town or the roads not being ploughed enough. Then, like every city council meeting you left, without hearing anything else that was going on." My dad paused in order to compose himself and to lower his tone. "I would have welcomed any ideas from anyone that would have meant we could have kept the price the same. But almost no one attends the meetings, and there was nothing else we could do."

"You know what you can do? You can tell me when my water will go back to normal." Ester gave a short glare and walked away.

My dad looked at me and rolled his eyes.

I wondered to myself, would he actually have listened at any of those city council meetings. Would he have listened to anyone who disagreed with him? I just didn't think so.

When Ester was at the end of the block I reluctantly walked inside my parent's house to talk to my dad.

"Hey Dad," I said.

"Have you heard any news about Jacqueline?" he asked, drinking his coffee and sifting through a large pile of paper. On the kitchen counter, the TV was turned to a conservative talk show.

"Yes, she got six months probation. They didn't feel it would be productive to put her in the big house. John was pretty happy."

My dad shook his head and rolled his eyes.

The voice from the talk show filled the silence. "It is these liberals; they want us all to accept everything. They want the gays to get married. Maybe they want people to be able to marry more than one person? The next thing you know they are going to be petitioning for adults to marry children."

"Oh my God, Dad, I want to marry two people. Oh, and I want to marry a cat also."

He gave me a sour look. "Sarah?"

After a short pause I said "Dad, people at the store have been complaining about what is going on around town, the water situation. It hasn't just been Ester."

"Well, if they are really that unhappy with what is going on, I suggest they get their asses down to the city council meetings. Or, they can move the hell out of town."

"Dad, there has to be something you can do?" I pleaded.

"You know what, Sarah?" my dad's tone quickly changed from tired to cantankerous. "The people in town need to stop acting like children. If they have an issue, they need to do something or come to me directly. I am not their daddy, I am not going to hand feed them every piece of information. People come to the city council meetings. The sad thing is, they expect you to fix everything, like I have some sort of magic wand. It irritates me that not one of the people who is doing the complaining actually comes with a solution."

"Ok, I love you Dad," I said, walking out the door. I noticed he kept the TV on the same station.

"Love you."

It turned out Douglas had recently acquired a great deal of free time because of a heating issue which had happened in the plant. Over Christmas, there had been some major damage to the Polar building, though Douglas didn't say specifically what the damage was, He really didn't want to tell me what happened. What I did know was that the plant was not in production. The water pressure had been almost back to normal since Christmas morning.

Douglas decided to put his free time to good use. In Minnesota, the coldest part of winter doesn't lend itself to many outdoor activities. As such, many individuals watch football and others catch up on their reading. However, the activity for the more masochistic residents who don't like to stay inside is to partake in is ice fishing. This was the activity Douglas talked me into.

The house Douglas had purchased in Ofiara came with a fish house in back. The same morning Ester accosted my dad, Douglas and I spent hours shoveling a path on the ice and pushing the small wooden room onto the lake. We placed it close to shore in shallow water, so as to up the odds of catching pan-fish. The truth was that neither of us had done a great deal of that type of fishing, but we looked on it as a chance to sit on the ice and drink some Schnapps.

Douglas and I drilled a hole with an auger, certain we would crack the ice and fall to an icy death under the frozen surface. Then we drilled a second hole. We were relatively happy when we didn't plunge into the icy water.

Finally, we were able to get to fishing. When we shut the door we noticed a strong musky smell, a reminder of warmer weather. I placed a worm on the end of my hook and Douglas went with his standard corn.

"I think we should move the entire town to Arizona," I said as the feeling was starting to leave my toes.

"It is so freaking cold," Douglas responded handing me a small bottle of cinnamon schnapps.

"I thought there was a heater in here?" I asked taking a drink.

"Yes," Douglas said excitedly and turned to the small propane heater in the corner. He walked over, switched it on, and turned back towards me. "You know, it is funny how someone can miss something directly in front of them."

Douglas sat back down. There were a few moments of silence and then came a repetitive crunching noise. I had a small flashback to Ester and hoped she had not come out on the lake as well. There was someone outside.

"What's that?" I asked in a whisper.

"Sounds like footsteps."

"What if it's a wolf?" I asked with my eyes getting wide, playing along.

"Or a sasquatch," Douglas grinned. His eyes got wide and he whispered, "Hide."

The door popped open and Jill peeked in. "This is where you are!"

"Come in," I responded urgently. "Hurry, you are going to let out whatever hot air we have in here."

"OK, OK!" Jill said, a little irritated at being rushed.

Danny followed Jill inside.

"Hola," Danny said.

With four of us in the fish house there was barely enough room to move. Jill leaned over and kissed me on the top of my head.

"Have you caught dinner yet?" she asked.

"No, we're working on staying alive in the bitter cold," Douglas said with a grin.

"So?" Jill said. "Did you have a chance to talk with your dad?"

Douglas gave me a questioning look.

"Jill and Danny want me to talk to my dad about the water situation," I said as I looked back towards Jill. "I did, but he got angry."

"Well, something is going to have to be done," Danny responded, sitting next to the small heater. "People are getting upset."

"Yes," Douglas said. "A small group of people is getting upset."

"I think there are more angry people than you think," Danny said as a counter-argument.

"I don't think so," Douglas said.

"I think some people are being a little erratic in the way they are approaching the situation," I replied.

"I'm not sure skyrocketing water prices and water pressure aren't reasons to get a little upset," Danny stated.

"Yes, I agree, but you always have the option of walking over to visit Donald yourself." I said with a little more defiance. "Right now, given the state of things, I don't see what else I can do."

"Sarah, are you kidding?" Danny asked, now mirroring my annoyance.

"No," I said defiantly.

"I don't think I'm wrong here Sarah," Danny said feeling a bit challenged.

I looked directly at Danny. "I never said you were wrong; what I said was that you can count me out of talking to my dad. Find another middleman."

"Do you honestly think you have no responsibility here?" Danny said in a loud voice.

"Your solution is to shut down Polar. What happens if Polar leaves and people don't have the money to pay for their mortgages and this place ends up as a ghost town? Are you going to protest that? Are you going to try and find out a solution for that Danny?" I asked.

"You're being a little dramatic Sarah," Jill said with a half grin. The kind of grin that implied she was irritated.

"Me?" I asked.

Douglas interjected. "I realize I have a lot on the line here, but I have to throw in my two cents. You guys are accusatory and defensive. And, with all due respect Danny and Jill, it seems a bit inane that you are pushing Sarah to talk to her dad. Why hasn't anyone come and talked to me? I live right next door. I have been trying as hard as I possibly can to find some sort of solution to the water issue and I really have had no assistance from anyone in town or anyone in the factory. Adding insult to injury, for months now I have had to put up with what can only be labeled as juvenile and childish antics."

"What exactly was it that we did?" asked Jill.

"Jill, I'm not an idiot. I was that person who used to do that crap," Douglas said. "Anyway, I'm out here ice fishing, in the bitter cold today because of something you did."

"If you are accusing us of something, I would like to know what it is," Danny said.

Chapter 28

Todd's trial started and ended on the same cold day at the end of January. His friends and family all stood in the court room, ready for a fight. It was a bit shocking when Todd pled guilty to the charges of felony theft. Because he pled guilty and settled on restitution he would get six months in county jail. There had been a videotape taken in the storehouse of the paper mill. The video clearly showed Todd putting large bags of methylcellulose on a dolly and hauling it towards the loading dock.

My heart sank as I watched him walk away. I looked over at Jill, Eric, and Jake. I wanted them to say something. I wanted all of us to say something. We were nothing more than cowards, and Todd going to jail, taking the fall for us was a bunch of crap. What we had done was pointless and Todd's fate was empty.

On the car ride back to Ofiara, I was so angry I couldn't talk to Jill.

"We can go visit him next week if he puts us on the list," Jill said, trying to break the silence. She looked out the window, drawing a thin line through the frost which gathered on the window.

"Todd made a choice, Sarah."

I kept looking forward. I was just angry.

It was hard to make love to someone I felt was not respecting my personal views and morals. I understood everyone involved with the adolescent style protests was more than aware of the risks, but they were tearing apart our little corner of the world. Everything I loved seemed to be turning into something different or evolving. I was staying the same and holding my ground. I didn't see a need for the change they engaged in and I was angry to be a part of it.

When we got back into town, I noticed some people in front of the utilities department holding signs. I was too angry and self absorbed at that moment to take a good look. I just wanted a nap.

Chapter 29

Information slowly leaked out about what had occurred on that bitterly cold Christmas Eve night at the Polar Beverage plant. Apparently, something went wrong with the computer system, the one which ran the buildings furnace. When the workers arrived in the morning after Christmas, they found a building flooded with water and mountains of ice. Most of the pipes in the building had giant cracks and holes, allowing the water to pour everywhere. No one could figure out what happened until Juan looked at the thermostat, only to discover it read eighty five degrees Fahrenheit. The word on the street was the computer had malfunctioned because the computer system had been built with a warmer climate in mind. I knew the computer system had been fucked with.

Douglas was on the receiving end of Peter's anger regarding the damage at the plant which cost well over a million dollars. Although insurance would cover a great deal of the damage, there was still the lost time on the production line. Most of the plant workers were forced to apply for unemployment, though some were able to help get the plant up and running. It was money lost for the town.

Eric came over to the store to help me move some shelves a few days after Todd's trial. My intention was to talk to him about what had happened at the Polar plant. He also had underlying motives.

Eric and I were pulling baking goods off a shelf, when he asked, "Is it just me or is there a bit of tension going on between you and Jill?"

"Wow that was out of the blue," I said, with an undertone of irritation.

"Hey, I'm just worried."

"Not your worry."

"Okies," he said.

"OK," I responded, cutting the subject off.

After a moment, I asked, "Eric, what did you guys do?"

"What do you mean?"

"At the plant? What did you do?"

"Sarah, this has nothing to do with you."

"Actually Eric, it had something to do with the entire town. If Polar had decided to close up, you would have been out of a job and so would around fifty people in town."

"Would that really be so bad?" Eric asked defensively.

"Yes Eric, yes, yes, yes! Do you realize what would happen to this town without Polar?"

"We would find a way," Eric said in a way which felt dismissive to me.

"You are sure of this?" I paused. "Do you have any idea how much ass-kissing Dad has had to do? The stunts you have been pulling?"

"Oh for God's sake Sarah, quit being so dramatic."

"If you are so fucking unhappy here, if you think you can do so much better someplace else, then just go someplace else. You don't have to drag this entire town down with you."

"You really think that is what it is?"

"Honestly, I don't know Eric. The difficulty I am having here is in how you are doing things. It doesn't look like some sort of effort to remove Polar. It looks and smells like revenge."

Eric turned and walked out of the store. It was rare for us to argue, partly because I knew Eric could hold a grudge for months.

Chapter 30

The second week of February people started coming into the store to buy their Valentine's Day cards. There had been several days when the weather was above average, causing water and ice to run down the streets to the lake. Though the weather was nice, it was difficult to keep the sidewalk in front of the store from becoming deadly slippery.

Norma and I walked in-between the shelves, completing a long overdue inventory of the store. It was supposed to be formally done every January. However, my procrastination was getting the better of me.

"We really do carry a great deal of inventory we don't even use," Norma said, looking over a clipboard she was holding.

I found a can of capers behind several jars of pickles and showed it to Norma. "Maybe we should put some of this stuff on sale, or even donate it to the food shelf."

"Nice thought, but I am not sure how kind it is to give the food no one else wants to those who are in poverty to begin with."

"Well, you know the saying beggars can't be..."

Norma cut me off. "Stop."

"What?" I asked. "If those people work hard enough, then they will be able to afford to pick and choose."

"I am one of those people," she said, looking at me. "And I have no damn idea what I would do with those capers."

I closed my eyes, realizing how rude what I said was. "Norma, I am so sorry."

"Sarah, it's OK," she said in a soft tone.

"No, no it's not. I'm sorry. For a moment I turned into my father."

Just then, a very tall woman with long dark hair walked into the store. I didn't get a good look at her. She made her way quickly to the produce section. She had grabbed some lettuce and walked back to the counter.

Making my way to the cash register, I peeked around the corner to catch a glimpse of the mystery Amazon woman. It took me a moment to figure out who the dark haired woman was. She seemed much more human than the first few times I had seen her. She actually seemed almost normal in jeans and a t-shirt.

"Janice? Janise Manson?" I asked. "You were Danny's lawyer."

She grinned. "I can't discuss clients."

"Are you here on work or for pleasure?" I asked.

"Visiting an old friend and a little work," Janice said with a cheeky smile. "Maybe I'll see you around." She then winked at me and walked out of the store.

My few moments of happiness were quickly replaced by animosity as Ester walked into the store. She was buying her same boring and bland food. I had always assumed it was some sort of masochistic or self-defeating behavior on her part. In essence, it was an attempt to make her life as lacking in flavor as possible. Of course, the staunch homophobe would not let the event such as Valentine's Day get by without saying something.

"Good afternoon, Ester," I said, trying to keep the conversation light.

Ester wasn't having any of it and went right for the jugular. "I certainly hope you have no intention of selling any of those fag Valentine's cards in your store Sarah?" she asked, fishing through her purse for the exact change. Sadly, none of that change would be going towards a card with colorful red hearts and a corny love poem. Ester had no valentine.

The most unusual purchase she made that day was a box of strychnine, which I guess could have been considered bizarre for anyone. Just like the capers I hadn't even realized there was such a product in the store.

"Ester, I am a businesswoman. If there was a demand for it in town, I would sell it. That is what I do. Unfortunately, as of yet, no one has asked for such cards. However, if there should ever be such demand, I will indeed sell lesbian and gay cards."

"Oh," she said, looking directly at me and raising one of her painted-on fake eyebrows.

Bonnie walked up behind Ester, giving me an apologetic smile.

"Carry this to my car and place it in the front seat," Ester said, pushing the bags towards me noxiously, as if I had no choice.

I smiled politely, picked up the bag, and carried it to her car.

"I hope this bag does not break," she said, opening her door.

"I think it will be fine, Ester. Just be careful not to let the poison mix with the rice." I smiled. "Have a good weekend, and maybe treat yourself a bit."

"Treat myself?" she said under her breath as I was walking away. "Like I am a damn dog. Come here Ester, good girl."

I walked back inside rolling my eyes when I was sure she could no longer see me.

Inside I rang up Bonnie's food and cleaning products. Bonnie placed her hand on mine. "You know there is a special place in heaven for people who are so kind to someone who acts with nothing but contempt towards them."

I paused and smiled "Thank you Bonnie."

"Sarah, do you know why people are hanging around outside the utilities department?"

"No. I'm a little ashamed to say I have no idea. In fact, when I drive past I don't even look."

"It reminds me a little of when the In-House plant workers went on strike."

It turned out Janice was Douglas' house guest. I was unable to get much information about why she was there, though this was most likely a good thing. I could feel myself starting to develop a crush.

It was a bad time for Janice to show up. Jill and I were struggling to get along. My resentment over what happened to Todd and at the Polar plant was getting exceedingly more difficult to deal with. Moreover, it made me angry that everyone seemed so unapologetic about all the destruction that had been caused.

Chapter 31

It didn't matter if Valentine's Day was kind to me or not. I loved the hearts, the flowers, and of course candy. It was the symbols and promises of something idealistic which usually ended up being better than the real.

There continued to be undertones of animosity between me and Jill. Neither of us was at the point of talking about the plethora of issues separating us. We weren't willing to compromise so we had to be content, at least for the time being, living in an emotional limbo. Our days were littered with moments where we did everything we could to casually avoid one another. It was a struggle I wanted gone, I wanted things back to normal.

Work felt like a good place to avoid home. I was sitting in my office trying my best to concentrate on the overdue accounts when my mom peeked inside my office.

"Hi," she said smiling.

"Hey mom."

"Happy Valentine's Day." She handed me a box filled with chocolates.

"Thanks mom!" I said opening the box and smelling the candy.

"Any exciting plans for tonight she asked?"

"We're staying at home. Dinner and a movie." I said not looking directly at her.

"Oh,"

"Hmmm," she looked at the floor "sounds really exciting."

"Mom?"

"Well, doesn't seem very romantic."

I leaned my head back and sighed. "Things are just a little confusing for me right now."

"How?" she asked.

"I really don't know how to explain it."

The truth was I knew, but if I told my mom she would tell my dad. My father would be less than happy to know about the damage Jill had inflicted on Polar. He would be even less happy if he knew about the close friendship which had formed between Jill and Danny. The truth had to be none of my dad's damn business.

My mother gave me one of her optimistic smiles. "In a relationship you aren't always going to see things the same."

"Oh mom, I know that." I returned her smile.

"Your dad and I have gone for months at a time being so angry at one another we could hardly speak. Really, talking is the only thing that solves the dilemma. As a couple, a pair."

Jill and I exchanged gifts that night. I gave her a colorful Swatch and she gave me a box of homemade chocolates. We could both feel something was missing and it wasn't just the sex.

Our standard intimacy replacement had become TV. Jill sat next to me on the couch occasionally touching my arm. It was frustrating because I knew my mind would eventually drift to sex. I would think about touching her, making love to her, and there would be no relief.

I did love Jill and I knew she loved me, of those two things I could be sure. It just wasn't clear if love was enough for either of us to trudge through the giant pile of crap we created to find out way back. We were missing respect for one another. Without respect there was no listening to one another.

Chapter 32

In the few remaining weeks of winter Jill and Danny had tried to enlist town residents in an effort to petition Polar Beverage. Their goal was to convince Polar to drastically reduce the amount of water they were using or close their doors for good. Only a handful of people signed and no one volunteered to help. It wasn't that those in Ofiara were somehow apathetic or didn't understand the impact of the water issue; rather, it was because the community was stretched a bit thin already. People had their own issues, their own problems. Moreover, there was also a small group of residents who didn't sign the petition because they or their family members worked for Polar. They were angry and acted rude towards Jill and Danny.

Repairs were done at the bottling plant and Polar Beverage had started up production. Sadly, water was again almost down to a trickle. Jill and Danny decided they would attend the city council meeting at the end of February hoping the difficulty with water pressure would add a little fuel to their fight. They brought their petition hoping for more support.

Scotty Thomson from the utilities department had also shown up to the meeting with at least one other employee of the city utilities department. They were sitting in the front row next to a very well dressed man. The well dressed man had a briefcase sitting on the floor next to him. My instincts told me the well dressed man was not trust worthy. There was just something I found particularly unsavory about a guy wearing an expensive suite in an area that was economically struggling. It also could have been his slicked back hair.

Ester was at the meeting as well. Her main concern was the continued issue with the stray dogs. She was angry no one had done anything about the problem and was now convinced they would spread disease around town. Of course, my dad would once again explain there was nothing he could do. She got angry and left.

It was Scotty's turn. He got up and walked to the podium studying a piece of paper just before he began to speak. "A week ago I sent a proposal out to all the council members. We think the price of water needs to be raised to fifty cents a gallon."

There was a rush of anxiety throughout my body. I was already stretched so thin between work and the store. It seemed impossible to try and come up with more money.

"That seems a bit steep." My dad said.

"There has to be some sort of incentive for people to curb their water use. Water levels aren't getting any better." Scotty paused and looked at my dad. "If water levels continue to decline we need to consider putting in another well." said Scotty.

"I think a new well is a discussion for another day." My dad asked

"I know that Don." Scotty said. "I wanted to emphasize we don't believe we can maintain the city well in its current location. The alternative is building a new well on the outskirts of town. A month ago I started making several phone calls about the water situation. Eventually I was contacted by Steve Brians from Universal Bank."

I heard Danny whisper "Oh fuck no." behind me.

Scotty continued "Mr. Brians explained to me there is a program through Universal Bank which was created to assist a communities like ours."

"What sort of a program?" asked my dad.

The well dressed man stood up "If you would allow me to explain."

"Mr. Brians I assume?" My dad asked.

"Yes." Steve Brians said. "We simply offer low interest loans for communities wishing to make improvements in their infrastructure. We also provide ongoing support to those communities we decide to invest in."

"Could you get a proposal to us?" asked my dad.

"Yes, I will get the names and addresses of council members after the meeting."

Scotty cut in. "I think we still need to raise water prices, just to be on the safe side."

My dad and the other council members leaned into a huddle whispering for a few moments then turned back to Scotty.

"We will very reluctantly start the increase to fifty cents a gallon starting March seventh."

Jill and Danny looked defeated.

That night when I got home I called Norma. I could hear the panic in her voice when I told her about the water prices going up.

I looked out my kitchen window and saw Janice walking into Douglas' house. She looked up at me and gave a half wave. I smiled back.

Chapter 33

I was so happy when St Patrick's Day arrived; honestly, I wanted to drink heavily.

Both my dad and Eric had dueling parties planned. I knew I had to make an appearance at my father's first, otherwise risk the silent treatment.

Jill and I arrived at my parent's house to find several of the town's businesspeople, the city council members, and other people who carried a label of influential in Ofiara. I'm not sure why but I was very surprised to see Peter there.

I felt sorry for Peter. I wondered how many other parts of himself he felt the need to hide from the world.

Douglas was there sitting and talking with my dad about something.

I hid out for a while in the kitchen with John making myself look busy with dishes and food. John was slowly getting tired of the party and talking about going over to catch part of Eric's shindig.

Peter walked into the kitchen. He looked unreasonably cocky.

John immediately looked over at me, his eyes telling me he wanted to see Peter removed.

"Well, hello Sarah," he paused "and John."

I realized Peter was attracted to John. Granted, John was a very handsome man, he was that dark hair brooding guy every girl in high school was absolutely in love with. However, I didn't think it was physical attributes that excited Peter; rather, it was the idea of corrupting someone with a good heart.

"Hello Peter," I replied.

John simply replied "Peter."

"How are things going at the store?" he asked in a way which implied he had zero investment in the answer.

"Good." I replied with even less enthusiasm than his.

"How's Jill?" He asked tilting her head to the side.

"She's good." I answered.

"Can I ask you something?" He looked over at a plate of cheese and grabbed a few slices.

"Sure," I said feeling a little sick in the stomach.

"Do you feel the presence of Polar Beverage has helped your store?" he asked shoving two pieces of cheese in his mouth at once.

I was distrustful of Peter. He was the type of manipulator who would latch on to any sign of possible weakness.

"Yes, in the overall scheme of things I guess you could say Polar Beverage has helped profits. However, if the water prices keep going up I'm scared that there won't be anyone in Ofiara who will be willing to buy anything from the store."

"Douglas is on the water pressure situation. I'm sure he will find a way to improve the water levels." Peter said picking through the crackers.

"What if that doesn't happen?" John asked with his back towards us looking out the window.

"It will happen," he smiled "You just got to have faith."

I could see Douglas watching the exchange through the corner of his eye.

"Faith? I am not sure faith has anything to do with it." John said looking straight at Peter this time. "The well is either going to replenish itself or it isn't."

"You think that God is going to abandon this small town then?" Peter asked a bit smug.

"Peter, with all due respect to whatever version of Christianity you practice I don't think God has anything to do with it."

I started feeling uncomfortable as I realized my dad was listening to the conversation as well.

"Why not?" asked Peter who also realized he had an audience at this point.

"Because praying for the water to be replenished in the well is like asking God to fix your toaster." John said.

"You don't believe God loves us enough to help is?"

"I believe that God is a good, kind, and loving God who loves all people. What I don't believe is that God is a magician. Putting that sort of label on God is what people do who want to create their own version of God rather than having the humility to say they could never comprehend God."

Peter gave John look of disapproval, the sort of look one gives letting a person know they have missed the entire point of the conversation.

Our visit had run its course and it felt like time to head over to Eric's party. I motioned Douglas to meet me outside. Jill grabbed John and the four of us headed out into what was a heavy but beautiful snowfall. I decided to ride with Douglas to help him find the way out to Eric's and Jill drove John.

"I seriously don't get this," I said fastening my seat belt.

"Don't get what?" asked Douglas starting the car and pulling away from the curve.

"You know, next to my father I was one of the biggest supporters of Polar moving into town." I sighed. "Douglas, did you know the water prices are going up?"

"Nope. How much?" he asked.

"Water will cost fifty cents a gallon." I shook my head and growled.

"Ouch."

"How about the loan from Universal Bank to drill a new well? Did you know about that?" I asked.

"No," said Douglas with a softened tone.

"Douglas, the town cannot afford to drill a new well and we certainly can't afford a loan to drill the well either."

"Sarah, we have become very good friends over the last few months, right?"

"Yeah, I would agree."

"Can I say something blunt without ruining our friendship?" he asked.

"Yes," I said hesitantly. I could see myself falling into the same trap I had fallen into just minutes prior in my dad's house.

"Pull your head out of your ass Sarah," he said with a smile.

"What?" I asked not really believing I had correctly heard what Douglas said.

"I can repeat it, if you would like."

"Nope, I think it has registered now." I said feeling my eyebrows crinkle.

"You know why this is happening? This is happening because people don't give a shit until things get really bad. Now that the price is high and is going to hurt your business you care."

"Umm, fuck you Douglas."

Douglas tilted his head a bit. "Sarah, you can't honestly be surprised."

"You're being kind of an ass hole Douglas." I pulled a bottle of beer out of my purse. "I thought you were supposed to be on the water situation Douglas."

"I'm trying my best." Douglas said.

I looked uncomfortably out the passenger side window guzzling down half my beer.

Douglas' words became empathetic. "Keeping our world good involves more than those things that are directly in front of us. It's not always going to be another group or person who is going to fix the problem and it sure as hell is not ever going to be a politician. You know why?"

"This isn't my fault." I asked with a sigh.

"Actually, it is your fault. If people would have said something, anything, when Polar and other countries where causing damage to other people and environments overseas they wouldn't think they can get away with it here. Peter wouldn't have been so aggressive with production."

"People who run companies are fairly well educated. I'm guessing they know the difference between crappy and appropriate behavior. Besides, I thought you were the guy who was going to make a better and more ecologically friendly bottling system?"

"I'm trying but it's a little difficult when there is absolutely no incentive for Polar to change the way they do things."

"OK, I'm not sure that explains why Peter has to be such an ass hole about things."

"Yeah," he said. "He is an ass."

I laughed.

"Sarah," he said sounding winded "Peter is a businessman. His job is to make money and it's a vocation he is quite good at. His job is not running a charity. If this plant does not make money, if there isn't good news, this plant gets closed. Peter is accountable to those people who have invested in Polar. If he fails, thousands of people lose money and fifty people lose their jobs."

I sighed "Douglas, he is doing a hell of a lot more than just trying to make money and keep jobs. He is instigating things," I looked at him "and the thing is you know it."

When we arrived Eric's house was packed with people. There was a haze of cigarette smoke and perhaps another type smoked material. The party was a fundraiser for Todd. Eric didn't want my dad to find out as our father now considered Todd nothing but a "common street thug." People placed donations into a jar as they walked in. There were several friends of Todd's who had driven from all over the state.

Douglas sat with Eric, Jill and I for quite some time. We were all doing shots of schnapps with beer. Of course, Eric was still icy towards me. He was still seething over the conversation at the grocery store. Unfortunately, my gut feeling was that the real reason was because he wanted to punish me and let me know it wasn't OK I wasn't as idealistic as him.

Jake was hanging out with a few girls, complimenting them on their hair and clothes. He was flattering them in all sorts of ways. They seemed to be eating up every word.

Danny came over and joined the group after several drinks. After a few moments I realized no one was really talking with me. I was more or less the ignored party in the conversation and decided to wander off.

I walked into the kitchen. That always seemed to be the room in most any house for which I would gravitate. A gimlet was calling my name. I looked to see if Eric had any gin hidden around the kitchen. Finding a bottle, in the back of a cupboard, behind the flour, I turned to the refrigerator for some ice.

"Hello," said a woman's voice just inches from me causing me to jump.

"Janice," I smiled. "Hey there."

"I'll take one of those as well." She grabbed a filbert and flipped it into her mouth.

Janice was wearing a white t-shirt and jeans with her hair down, she looked beautiful.

I didn't want to be rude but I had to ask "How did you get out here?"

"Norma gave me a ride." she said.

I dumped two handfuls of ice into two glasses then poured about three shots worth of gin in each glass. It wasn't normal for me to make a drink that strong, but I was so nervous. I tried hard to hide the fact my hands were shaking as I carefully poured in the lime juice.

"How are you enjoying our little town?" I asked.

"Actually, I like it. Sometimes, it's nice to slow down a little." She replied.

She had started to look directly at me in this intense way. She had these big brown eyes that almost looked black. She placed her hand underneath mine and looked at a silver band I had on my index finger. I wanted to kiss her right there, in the middle of the kitchen.

"This is beautiful." She said pulling the ring close to her face and looking at it. While she studied the ring her thumb massaged the palm of my hand.

"Where did you get it?" she asked as my brain filled with the image of kissing her.

"South Dakota, I went there on a trip with some friends once."

"Hello." Jill's voice suddenly came from behind giving me a shot of guilt right in the heart. Jill was stone cold drunk to the point here eyes were opening and closing slowly.

"Hey," I said both happy and sad the moment had ended. "Oh Jill, this is Janice. She was Danny's lawyer.

As Jill made her way across the kitchen she had to stop twice, swaying slightly.

"Yes, aren't you the one staying with Douglas?" Jill asked.

Janice nodded "Douglas and I have been friends for years. He was nice enough to let me stay at his house while I am doing some work in the area." Janice smiled and shook her head. "It seems as though the crime rate keeps going up around these parts."

"Well, that is very true." Jill said. "Sarah, I am not feeling well. Can we go home?"

"Of course," I said realizing too many shots of tequila had made her look a little green.

"Another time," I said with a whimper of defeat.

As we were leaving I turned to see Janice watching us walk out the door. I felt guilty for the thoughts I had about Janice but at the same time it felt good. It was awesome feeling that rush of emotion, the excitement of the undefined and indefinite.

Chapter 34

A few days after the St. Patrick's Day festivities the small group of people with signs outside the utilities department finally caught Ofiara's attention. Shoppers coming in and out of the grocery store talked constantly about it assuming then drawing conclusions. Some individuals said they supported the protesters while others thought it was stupid. I didn't really think most people knew what was happening. Regardless of whether or not town residents understood they all seemed to have an opinion.

The protesters seemed concerned with the current water prices and afraid they might increase even more. They wanted to see the price go down to a manageable level. Fifty cents a gallon was just too much to pay for water.

Some people from in town would drive past the spectacle picking out the individuals they recognized. There were onlookers that would just gawk while others would yell or honk their support. The loud horn supporters didn't join the line. They wanted to support the protesters, but only on their terms.

There were also the individuals who decided they just had to be jerks. They would holler at the protesters to get a job or to get a life. Some people called them losers while others called them leaches on society who simply wanted a free ride, someone else to pay their way. Perhaps those rude and angry people really felt they had something to say about the protesters. What they ended up doing was saying something about their self.

There were a few workers from the beverage plant that made a special point of making things difficult for the protesters. One person who came into the store laughed a little when he told me Sam had thrown garbage at the protesters. I thought about how rude Sam could be, but of course I said nothing.

My dad said that if the people were protesting worked harder or tried to get a better job, they would not have been in the situation they were in. He said that in the United States everyone has the same opportunities in life and some people just chose to squander theirs. It just didn't make sense to my dad that people born in the same country would not be able to catch their dreams.

I felt a bit of kinship with the protesters as my water bill was now close to two hundred dollars a month. In fact, every person in town was struggling with the inflated cost of water. The protesters were no different with one exception, they were doing something.

Water prices were far from the biggest issue on my mind. Things weren't any better between Jill and I. There was a pervasive silence regarding the issues that mattered most. I didn't feel as though Jill had either heard or understood my feelings in general. It was clear that she wanted me to take an active role in fighting Polar Beverage and trying to get them to either fix things or move out of town. When one of us came close to bringing up the topic, an invisible wall of defensiveness would grow directly in the middle of the room, and we would both retreat to our separate corners.

The avoidant solution for what was going on between Jill and I seemed to be increasing my time at the grocery store. I had started to work ten to twelve hour days, sometimes seven days a week. Avoiding the problem may have been a short term solution but it sure as hell seemed better than confrontation.

"Nice bracelet." Norma said to Terry as she was ringing up her groceries.

I was listening in from a few isles away while stacking soup on the shelves. I would have walked over but just was not in the mood for an argument or a fake truce, either one would have taken too much energy. I could see the both of them clearly from a round mirror placed in the back corner of the store.

"Thank you," Terry responded.

"Was it a gift?" Norma asked.

"I decided that I deserved something pretty." Terry said pushing her arm towards Norma so she could get a better look.

"Well, it is very nice." Norma said as Terry grabbed her bag and walked out the door and into her new SUV.

I walked with some empty boxes up to the counter just in time to see Terry driving away past the storefront window.

"Wow," Norma said. "Maybe I should be going into law enforcement rather than mortuary science. What the hell are they paying deputies these days?"

"I have no damn idea." I said with a slight laugh.

"That women has all the subtly of a cat with tape stuck to its back paw." Norma said grabbing a rag and whipping of the counter.

The door opened and Janice walked through the front. It was difficult for me to look directly at her because when I did my face would go red. She was the island of happiness in my head which I would swim to in the darkness of sleep.

"Good morning ladies," Janice said with a big smile.

"Hey Janice," Norma said.

"Hello Janice," I said with puppy like grin.

"Norma, I wanted to ask if it would be OK for us to meet later in the week." Janice asked pointing towards a pack of cigarettes.

Norma put her finger on a pack of American Spirit and Janice nodded in approval.

"Not a problem, I am a little busy with getting a paper done for a class. I also have a project where I am planning a funeral." Norma replied.

"I didn't picture you a smoker." I said to Janice.

"Yeah?" Janice said.

"It's just that you don't look like a smoker." I said realizing I was digging myself into a hole.

"What does a smoker look like?" She asked.

"Tough and mean?" I said with a smile.

I loved that feeling I got when Janice was around the excitement of a crush. What I didn't like was knowing I was close to a line that couldn't be crossed. If I tried too hard to get what I wanted I would lose what I already had.

Chapter 35

The April weather was so warm most people didn't wear jackets. Snow was melting quickly. The unfortunate by-product of the nice weather was that the town had an unwashed, unclean, dirty smell, which penetrated every structure in town. Mud was everywhere. Most residents couldn't afford the water it would take to be constantly washing out the entry way of their homes and businesses.

It wasn't just floors and entryways it was also Laundry. Clothing wasn't washed as often as it had been in the previous years. Most parents in town were very frustrated. They felt, kids walking around with dirt on their clothes, was an indication of bad parenting.

The protesters continued their presence at the water plant though their numbers hadn't increased by much. I wasn't sure why, but for weeks I was scared to look too closely at the protesters. The conflict frightened me. When I finally started actually looking at the individuals protesting I realized Norma was one of them. I would often see her there before and after work or school, marching with her sign saying "What don't you get, we cannot afford this."

A few people continued their work harassing the protesters. Many of the individuals doing the harassing continued to drive past and shout things. The only evolution made in their thoughts or actions being their language becoming more violent and graphic. It was as though they were angry the protesters were not stopping and not backing down from the point they were trying to make. The reality was that life can be grossly unfair to some people, regardless of what side of the argument an individual fell on.

Jill's parents and sister had come to stay with us for Easter. We had prepared the two spare bedrooms for their arrival. Jill had planned several days of food, shopping, and of an Easter Celebration at my dad's house.

Truth be told, I was happy to have other people staying with us. I needed a break. We both needed some sort of respite from the ongoing animosity in the house. We needed to either start talking or visit with a therapist. Our issues were not going to just magically work themselves out. Unfortunately, I couldn't see either of us willing to swallow our pride or even attempt to say something.

The day before Easter is always busy in the store with people getting last minute items. Most of those who lived in Ofiara knew the store was not open on Easter Sunday. They also knew that regardless of how many times they called my house on Easter Sunday I wasn't going to open up. I wouldn't compromise on a vacation day.

Peter came into the store early that morning with his wife. The first thing that went through my head was the night Jill and I witnessed his interlude with a man outside his townhouse. Seeing him together with his wife was vastly different than I had thought. They laughed and flirted with one another as they walked through the store, looking for something to bring to my parents house for Easter dinner. Although he seemed much more human in the context of the store I couldn't help but grimace.

After work I stopped at Douglas' house. He was getting things packed up to drive down to his mom's for Easter. He said the main reason Peter's wife was in town for Easter was so he didn't have to leave. He needed to keep an eye on the plant while Douglas went home. Since the frozen pipes incident Peter's trust level had gone way down.

"Sarah!" Douglas yelled as I walked up the driveway.

"How's it going?" I asked looking around.

"Well, I am glad to be going away for a few days." He said as he put a bag in the trunk of his car.

"So, is Janice watching your house while you are gone?" I asked.

"Clean up the shit in one yard before you move on to another Sarah." Douglas said with an almost stern tone.

"Umm, I am not sure what you mean Douglas."

"Sure you do." He said closing the trunk. "Hey, Janice is a very attractive woman. However, you should really take care of what is going on between you and Jill before you try and enter another relationship."

"Yeah?" I asked with an annoyed tone in my voice.

Douglas hugged me. "Sarah, I know you want to avoid what is going on, because it will temporarily be easier. However, the longer you wait the more difficult the decision will be one way or another."

Douglas was right, and I was too ashamed to admit it.

Chapter 36

Easter Sunday arrived giving me my well deserved day off. Jill had walked over to my parent's house early to help my mom. A few hours later I walked over with Jill's family.

Eric and Danny were very warm towards Jill's family as was my mom. My dad was a different story. It wasn't that he was rude; I think it was because he was not ready to meet his daughter's girlfriend's family. He realized my being gay wasn't just some kind of passing fad was just too much for him. He could accept me and Jill, but not the absolute idea of true love. He decided to stay outside with his grill, where there would not have to deal with the situation.

Regardless of my dad's reservations I decided to enjoy the day.

Jason and his mom arrived shortly after me and Jill's family. Everyone was dressed up except for Jason who decided to wear jeans and a t-shirt. Jason had brought Monet with. However, my dad didn't allow Monet to come in. My dad then warned Jason that if Monet was to make any sort of mess Jason would be the one to clean up the mess.

Walking into the kitchen to get a glass of wine I stopped and looked at Jill. She was wearing a pink halter dress with a white sweater. Everything about her looked beautiful. It was in that moment I understood I couldn't give her up. I walked over and smiled grabbing her by the hand and pulling her to the front porch.

"I love you," I said with a serious tone.

"Yes," she said with a smile "I love you to."

"But, I don't believe what you did was right."

Jill rolled her eyes a little "Sarah, let's not do this now."

I sighed "If we are going to try and make things work we are going to have to try and do something."

"I agree, but seriously, this is not the time."

"We need to make some time and actually talk. I am not sure either one of us is ever going to believe the other is right, but we have to find a middle ground."

Jill leaned over and hugged me then pulled back giving me a kiss. "Yes."

"Jason?" I heard my mom yell from the next room.

"Yeah?" he responded.

My mom continued "I just got a call from John. He's going to be a few minutes late after church. Can you pick up Jacqueline?"

About twenty minutes after Jason drove over to pick up Jacqueline for dinner he called my parents house in a panic. My dad and I drove over to find Jason standing by an ambulance. He was watching as two EMTs had started to pack Jacqueline away in a zipped body size bag.

Jason said that he knocked and knocked, then walked around the side of the house, looking into the windows. He saw Jacqueline on the kitchen floor. The ambulance driver told Jason she had a heart attack and there would have been little anyone could have done to help.

John arrived just as they were about to close the doors. He was wearing his white collar slightly unbuttoned.

"One moment please." John said with tears in his eyes.

John stepped up into the back of the ambulance and unzipped the black plastic bag. He took one hand and ran it over Jacqueline's hair and gave her a soft kiss on the forehead.

"Bye." He said with his hands shaking and tears flowing from his eyes.

Chapter 37

It was warm and sunny the day Jacqueline was laid to rest. Jacqueline had made her funeral arrangements in advance, purchasing a plot, a coffin, and even picking out the readings and music for her service. She had also ordered white flowers of all kinds for the service.

Jacqueline placed Norma in charge of carrying out her wishes. It was the first time Norma had planned a funeral from start to finish. It was something special and something to put on her resume.

John presided over the service, which I didn't completely agree with. He said she would have wanted that way. John also said that because there was such a shortage of priests in the area, there really wasn't another option. I thought he was a little full of shit on both points, but I wasn't about to argue with him.

It seemed as if everyone in town showed up for the funeral. My dad claimed people showed up for the free food. I didn't want to have an opinion on people's intentions.

In traditional Ofiara fashion, several residents, myself included, stayed up all night telling stories and giving testimonials about Jacqueline. We laughed at some stories and cried at others. All the while, John stood clear of most of the groups of people.

The morning following the funeral, there was another protest of sorts. On my way to work, I looked down the road to see the protesters had moved to the front of the Polar Beverage Plant. Strangely, the small crowd wasn't doing anything; they were just looking down at the gravel road. As I walked closer, I saw the area around the road was littered with several empty spray paint cans. Someone, perhaps a young artist, had covered the road with what looked like a painted river. Throughout the currents of dry water were the words, "Stop before it's too late."

I looked around to see if Jason was still there, but it appeared he had exited the scene of the crime. I did see Douglas directly across the road from me. He was trying to hold back a grin.

"It's beautiful!" I yelled across the road.

"Yes it is," he said with a nod and walked off.

The very public defamation of Polar was not the only indignity the corporation would suffer in Ofiara in April. Danny was given a list of names from Matt Bergen. The list held the names of the corporate board members and share holders. Matt had told Danny that the list was hers to do with what she wanted, but he made a recommendation, that she send out letters to the board members and share holders and let them know the cost at which their profits at Polar were being made.

Chapter 38

In May, everyone in Ofiara seemed agitated. Half the town wanted Polar Beverage gone and never to return. The other half wanted the protesters to just shut up and go away. Each side felt certain they had the answers which would save Ofiara. The one certainty was that each side was not listening to the other.

Making things even worse, equipment had been brought in for work on the new well meant specifically for Polar Beverage. Those who were struggling to pay their water bills felt angry Polar would end up taking even more water. Additionally, there had been whispers around the store. People were talking about a number of households where the water had been shut off. When I heard this, it was especially frightening, because I didn't see myself all that far off from being part of the group that no longer had water.

Those who worked at the plant looked at the drilling as job security. The added well meant they could continue to produce and the plant would continue to employ them. The individuals who depended on the plant for an income knew if something happened to Polar it would be bad for all of them. If the bottling plant had to either lay people off or close its doors, people could lose everything they had worked so hard for. They could fall behind on credit cards, lose their homes, and worst of all was the idea of having to ask a charity for financial help. It was more than the idea of losing everything; it was the fear of the humiliation which accompanies poverty.

Aside from those who were either so starkly against Polar or behind it, there was yet another group. This group was made up of the men, women, and children who stood outside protesting every weekday. They continued to hold signs, trying to get people to listen. All they wanted was someone to listen. Some people ignored them while others yelled things at them.

Chapter 39

The Friday morning which started Memorial Day weekend I walked outside to be greeted by hot dry air. It was only a few minutes after six in the morning and it already felt like eighty degrees. It was going to be a hot summer.

Douglas was walking into his yard and looked over and gave me a wave. He had started taking early morning walks. I think it was because he was starting internalizing everything that was going on with the people in town and Polar. He was leaving sometime in the early morning and getting home at around six am. A few mornings I had walked over and put either cookies or fresh coffee on his step. I just couldn't imagine being in his shoes, but I sure as hell was glad I wasn't.

Unlocking the door the Friday I looked down toward the lake. Normally I would wish for the tethers of work to be gone and the freedom to pursue my dream as a beach bum. That year I was only wishing things would go back to normal in Ofiara. It took a moment for me to realize I was watching Norma walk up the hill from the lake. She was walking with her two children dressed in robes. She carried a bucket of what looked like shampoo and conditioner.

I waved to Norma. She gave me a half wave back, looking a little embarrassed. My heart sank when I realized what was happening.

"How's Norma this morning?" I asked, knowing full well this was a dumb question.

"I feel a little embarrassed," Norma said, looking down.

"Norma, you should have told me. I'm sure there is something I could have done."

"That's sweet Sarah, but it has become a little difficult to imagine counting on others in town."

"What happened?" I asked, not knowing if I was sure I wanted to hear the answer.

"When the price of water went up I tried to lower the amount of water I used, but it wasn't enough. My water bill ended up being a little over five hundred dollars. At the beginning of April, I had close to eight hundred dollars outstanding at the utilities department. I ended up having to go to social services, and was sent to a non-profit. The non-profit gave me a grant, but made sure to let me know it was ridiculous for me to let my bill get so high. They also told me they would not help again."

"Oh Norma, I am so sorry." I felt as though I was crawling out of my skin with discomfort. I felt both ignorant and arrogant. It had not occurred to me to think past myself.

Norma smiled and rolled her eyes a bit, passing it off as something that was just a normal part of life. "I've been able to get my water usage to a little under a hundred and fifty gallons a month, but it is still a hardship. I only take a shower twice a week and the kids get a bath at that same time. We don't always flush the toilet, if you know what I mean," she laughed. "With cleaning I still use about the same amount of water, but I have to bring my laundry into a Laundromat in Grand Rapids once a week, otherwise it is too expensive."

"This isn't right Norma," I said, my heart sinking.

"Oh Sarah," Norma said giving me a hug. "It is nice to get some sympathy from someone. But, I have to tell you, there are people who are going through much worse. Many of my neighbors have had their water turned off for a few months now."

"What do they do?" I asked

"Well, before the snow melted, they were able to use it. However, they had to melt it and then boil it for most uses. Some of the residents have been going to the lake early in the morning or the middle of the night and getting buckets of water. That way they can flush their toilets, do dishes and take at least a sponge bath."

"Why hasn't anyone said anything?" I asked.

"Sarah, we have been saying things. We have been protesting for months, trying to get people to understand, but no one wants to listen. We have talked to your dad and he tells us that his hands are tied. We have tried to contact the head of the utilities department and he tells us that it is not his decision. We have tried to get people's attention and no one would listen."

I realized she was right, no one had been listening. Norma and her neighbors had been screaming for help. Unfortunately, residents did not seem to see the issue at hand. I was proof of this. When I drove past, I hardly looked at the picketers. I did not really bother to find out what they had to say. Honestly, I wasn't listening too much of anything, other than my fear of a failing business.

"But having your water shut off and having to take water from the lake? That is bad. You know the resort and cabins around the lake only stopped dumping raw sewage about twenty years ago?" I said, realizing my stomach was getting sick on top of the discomfort with the conversation.

"Yes, very aware of that, Sarah," Norma said with a smile. "You know, a problem like this is a lot like death. People go into denial, sometimes for a long period of time. Then, when they do finally settle on what has happened, it is usually their version and not the stark reality. I just don't think people want to know the truth. Instead, they would just like to go on with their lives."

"What can I do, Norma?"

She grinned and grabbed me by the arms, looking me dead in the eyes. "You can get your ass down to where we are protesting. If you don't feel comfortable protesting, you can maybe help us some other way."

Shortly after I opened, John wandered into the store. In the weeks since his mother died he had more or less thrown himself into his work, and it was rare to see him out of his collar. I would visit him most days and he would tell me he was doing well. Really, he wasn't. He looked as though someone had hollowed him out and replaced his insides with sand.

"Hey," he said, making only as much eye contact as was needed.

"How are you doing?" I asked.

"Actually, I think I am doing a little better."

"How do you mean? How are you doing better?" I asked, turning my head slightly. It wasn't that I doubted what he was saying; sadly, it was because I wanted him to prove it to himself.

"This morning, as I was getting ready, I was actually thinking about what I was doing. It wasn't just some sort of set-in structure in my life. It was like I had started to wake up from a nightmare."

I walked over to a table in the front of the store and poured a cup of coffee the both of us. "I wish this hadn't happened, John."

"I know," John said, taking a drink from the cup. "Oh Sarah, when are you going to learn how to make a cup of coffee?"

"My coffee is awesome John."

"It is terrible," he said.

"Nope," I said, sitting on the counter.

"By the way, I have it on good authority Terry has been suspended."

My eyebrows scrunched together. "Really, how did you find that out?"

John simply gave me the look. It was the look that implied I needed to stop asking questions.

Chapter 40

When I finally left work the Friday of Memorial Day weekend I went for cocktails with Douglas and Jill. We went to the restaurant next to the grocery store so we could sit out on the patio. It was so beautiful, at dusk, looking out over the lake. I tried to enjoy the view, but my mind drifted back to the family dressed in housecoats coming from the lake.

Jake's dad was the owner of the restaurant. It had been in their family for years. I always assumed that when Jake was able to come up with the money, he would buy it from his dad and it would be his.

Todd walked over to the table. He had been released from Jail the Monday prior and looked more than happy to be out.

"Todd!" I yelled and jumped up giving him a hug.

"Hey there, cats and kittens," Todd said with a smile.

"Pull up a chair," Jill smiled.

"I can't, I am working," Todd replied.

"And what is it you are doing?" I asked.

"Until I can find another job, I am working here. Jake's dad put me to work as a bartender. Honestly, I like it. Which reminds me, were you going to order or did you just come in to harass the help?"

"Three Coronas please, Barkeep." Douglas said to Todd.

"One thing, have you noticed there aren't a lot of locals in here?" Todd asked.

"Yeah, but I thought that was because this is the onset of tourist season," I said.

"No, prices went up a bit," Todd said, holding his hands up. "I'm just trying to forewarn you."

"How much did they go up?" Jill asked.

"The three beers are going to cost fifteen buckaroos," Todd said, closing one eye like he was expecting to be hit by a flying table.

"Wow, kind of steep wouldn't you say?" Douglas asked.

"Jake's dad doesn't really have a choice. With the cleaning and dishwashing, the water bill is high. If he doesn't raise the prices, he can't stay in business."

"I think we need the beer." Douglas said.

Todd walked to the patio bar and pulled out three beers.

"Damn it." Douglas said fishing around his wallet. "This fucking sucks."

"Our water bill is about two hundred and fifty dollars a month," I said.

"Hmmm," said Jill. "I wonder who is to blame for this?"

"Jill?" I said "Just for tonight fucking let it go."

Danny and Eric walked in and pulled up chairs.

"Oh bartender would you bring us a round?" Eric asked, with a wave to Todd. He then whispered, "It's hard to get good service."

"You all were having a party and didn't invite us?" Danny asked.

"The both of you are like homing pigeons when it comes to drinking; we just sort of assumed you would show up," I said with a grin.

Eric made a face at me and said, "Ha, ha, and ha!"

"Yeah, I thought it was funny," I responded.

Todd brought all five beers at once, balancing them against his chest. "OK Eric, that will be thirty dollars."

"No it won't, its twenty five," I said, scrunching my eyebrows together.

"Yeah, with Eric you have to include the tip," Todd said in a serious tone.

Eric handed Todd some bills. "Thank you for your patronage, kind sir," Todd said with a smile and a bow and walked back to the bar.

"You guys getting anywhere on your efforts to close down Polar?" Douglas asked looking at Danny then at Jill.

"We're still working on it," Danny said.

"That shareholders list doing you any good?" Douglas asked, causing Danny to cough a little into her beer.

Jill said coyly, "Well, whatever do you mean?"

"You know, I hate to rain on your parade. The shareholders are not going to give a flying rat's ass about a small town in Minnesota. Yes, a few of them made some phone calls, but really, all they care about is the bottom line. The bottom line is profits," Douglas said with an undertone of arrogance.

"Yeah, I'm not sure they'll feel the same way when we call the media," Jill said.

"Indeed," said Douglas, playing with a lime, "then they will care for the thirty seconds the story airs on the news, and they will go back to their portfolios."

"I don't think people are that callous," Jill responded in her ever optimistic way.

"I agree," said Douglas. "I think for the most part people are really good. The difficulty is that we live in a busy world where people have to pick their causes and battles. A person will care about the issue and maybe even express anger, but they have their own battles in their own lives to contend with. Why exactly do you feel that the issues of water in a small town in Minnesota are more important than their problems?"

"I think we're going to bring you down," Danny said.

"Why is it that I don't see the both of you hanging out with the protesters?" I asked.

Danny simply looked at me as though I was speaking a language she did not understand.

After a short pause Jill finally answered, "They're protesting not being able to pay their bills. That is not the issue we are having."

"Wow," Douglas said, rubbing his hands on his face. "You don't see that you have a common goal with the protesters at the utilities department?"

"Douglas, those people are living in the trailer park for a reason," Eric responded.

"Those people?" Douglas replied, obviously offended. "I grew up in a trailer park."

"Norma lives in that trailer park," I responded.

"Well, maybe not all of them, but quite a few of them are not known for being the most responsible people in town," Danny said, matching the defensive tone of Douglas.

"How many of 'those people' do you know?" Douglas asked.

"It's a small town, we know almost everyone," Eric said.

"OK, let me rephrase this; how many of the individuals in the trailer park do any of you spend time with?" Doulas asked.

"We run into them all over town all the time. We see them at the beach, at the store, and the gas station," Eric responded.

"How often do you talk to them? I mean do you have any idea what is going on in their lives?" Douglas asked. "A couple of the people who work at the plant also live in that trailer park. Those guys work their butts off on the line. I guess I am hard-pressed to see a difference between them and you all."

It was at that point in the conversation that I had to at least offer some back-up for Douglas. "I talked to Norma this morning. Did anyone here know that several of the residents at the trailer park have had their water turned off? They are the ones suffering most from the water issue."

"There are two major differences between the individuals at the trailer park. The first one is luck and the second is opportunity. With the exception of me everyone at this table came from a family that was either middle class or upper middle class. Your families had more options and connections." Douglas was clearly getting pissed off.

"Hey, I have earned everything I have," Eric responded.

"Don't you have a criminal record, Eric?" Douglas asked Eric. "Do you really think you would have gotten a job at the plant had your dad not been a connection? Do you think Todd would have a job right now if it wasn't for his connections? Also, Danny, my guess is that if you did not have Eric right now, you would also be living in that trailer park or with your mom. You both have made decisions that would have damned a person born into a family in poverty. Jill, you came from a very upper class family, you would have had to forcefully try not to be a success."

"What about you Douglas? You are managing a beverage plant with several employees," Jill replied.

"I got lucky. It was luck, pure and simple."

"So, does this have a point?" asked Jill, also annoyed with Douglas.

Douglas stood up and said, "Yes, if the lot of you plan on creating any sort of change, I would strongly advise you crawl down off the pedestal on which you have placed yourselves and work with those individuals from the trailer park. They're not beneath you and you are not better than them."

My mom, Jill and I walked to the Memorial Day Parade, which was set to start at ten in the morning. There were even fewer people at the parade that year despite the fact there were troops returning home from the Middle East. Watching the uniformed soldiers made my heart heavy. In the course of every moment, there is so much unseen pain in the world. Things I could never in a million years, conceptualize, or understand. Pain that damages people over and over.

I heard the sound of clapping next to me. I looked over to see Jill cheering on the soldiers. My pacifist anti-war girlfriend was paying her respects to the men and women as they walked down the street. Before I knew what was happening, my mom was also clapping. Slowly, the noise spread up and down both sides of the street. Jill was thinking outside of herself.

Brian Kirkpatrick drifted through my brain. I wondered if John had ever found out why Brian's mother kept crying. I wondered where Brian was.

After the parade Jill and I went for a walk. I steered us towards the trailer park. I hadn't been there in years and thought it would be a good idea to see for myself. We made our way past Polar and a few other odd buildings and hit the trailer park.

A few days prior my dad had told me at least eight homes in the trailer park had their water turned off because they had not paid their bills. He said that if people want their water they need to figure out how to budget. My father didn't feel water is a human right. I had to wonder as Jill and I wandered between trailers, if my dad had ever been to the trailer park. I loved him dearly and respected him to no end but I did realize he wasn`t the type of person who could understand something unless he experienced it.

Next to many of the trailers were buckets with different types of funnels on top meant to catch the rain. There was little or no grass between each of the homes. In a few spots there was the distinct smell of raw sewage, as though it had simply been thrown out.

I started seeing things I had not seen before. I would see someone walking down the road to the lake with a five gallon bucket and I would realize what that bucket was for. If someone came into the store smelling bad, I would think about how they most likely couldn't afford the water. It was the realization that, perhaps, I did not know what other people were going through. Maybe, without being in another person's shoes I could not make assumptions about the possible solutions that did or did not exist in their lives.

Chapter 41

Only a few days into June, Norma called in sick to work, which was rare. She was not calling in because she was sick or something had happened to one of her kids. Instead something had happened to her neighbor Anna.

Anna's five year old son Coal hadn't been able to eat or drink for two days. Every time Anna tried to give him something, he would throw it up. He was also suffering from chronic diarrhea. On the second day, his mother noticed his breathing was labored. She packed him up and headed for Grand Rapids. One hour and ten minutes after she arrived with her son, he passed away. The doctor said it was dehydration.

Norma told me Anna had been taking buckets of water from the lake and using it for things like cleaning. Anna caught Coal drinking out of one of the water buckets, but didn't think much about it until he became sick the next day.

Norma was right. The water issue may have affected me, but it was still at a point that was somewhat tolerable. Perhaps that was why I decided to stay uninvolved for so long. The more and more I thought about it, the more I realized something important. Eventually this would affect me.

The price of water was going up again; this time it was increased to seventy five cents a gallon. The utilities department and the city council had made this outrageous decision for two reasons. First, a price increase of this magnitude would force people to use much less water. There must have been a definitive failure in communication at some point, because no one seemed to understand how critical the water situation had become. People had continued to utilize much more water than they needed, sometimes as much as 400 gallons. Even though this number was half of what it was a year before, it still wasn't low enough. The second reason was that Ofiara was at a point where they would have to seek alternatives to the current system. The town was looking at alternatives such as building a new well or collecting and storing ground water.

Regardless of the water scarcity, at the end of June, there was a slight rise in water use. Workers at the utilities department were not able to account for the extra usage. Like all good managers, the utilities manager decided that he would check out the water meters around town. Scotty spent the last week of the month going from house to house, being chased by dogs, and climbing fences. He did it all in the name of accountability. When he reached the trailer park he found something strange. Of the twenty seven homes in the trailer park, twenty five had broken meters. Additionally, several people around town whose water had been shut off had it turned back on again. Someone had cut the locks on the valves and simply turned them back on.

It occurred to me Douglas was behind the broken meters and locks. However, he would never fess up to his actions. I don't think it was that he was afraid of getting into trouble; it was that he wasn't the type to take credit for something, anything he did.

Many of the people Douglas supervised at the plant had taken a different stance on the protesters. In fact, a small group of Polar employees had taken it upon themselves to talk with the protesters. One Friday at the beginning of June several Polar workers led by Sam, the shift manager from the plant, decided to defend their plant from the protesters. They felt the protesters were just trying to take away their livelihood.

After a few minutes, the talking turned into heckling. Moments after that one of the protesters and one of the workers started pushing each another. Norma tried to get between the two men in an attempt to stop whatever violence they had in mind. The violence ended up exploding on Norma's cheek. Dean, who had also joined the protest, grabbed both men by the back of their necks and pushed them to their knees. He very politely explained to the two men, a third his age, that the violence would not repeat itself. The plant workers left, indignity by their sides.

Jill and Danny were very busy collaborating with the protesters. Janice had assigned the two women the task of spending their spare time calling the media as well as political offices. The story hadn't gathered as much attention as hoped.

The calls made by Jill and Danny had attracted a handful of politicians. When the political figures came to Ofiara they held meetings at our town hall and spoke in optimistic ideas. One congressman wanted us to filter and use the lake water for household use.

At another meeting a state representative had yet another solution. In a hot and very overcrowded town hall, he told us he felt the town should apply for a grant to drill a deeper well. He was excited to say a bank had already met with him and would OK a loan guaranteed by the federal government. My father looked on with curiosity at this idea; his interest had been sparked. It seemed like a viable solution. It was almost the exact same sales pitch which had occurred a few months earlier at the city council meeting.

Danny raised her hand at the back of the room, "Representative Davis."

"Yes, the young woman in the yellow shirt," he responded, pointing at her.

"What sort of strings will be attached to this deal?" Danny asked.

My dad rolled his eyes and turned away out of frustration.

"What do you mean?" asked Representative Davis.

Danny took a deep breath. "Sometimes these loans come with strings attached."

The politician's voice went up slightly. "Strings?"

My dad turned and walked out of the room with me close behind.

"Dad, she is just scared. She is scared something bad is going to happen."

My dad looked straight at me and said, "You know what Sarah, not everyone agrees with your lifestyle. You don't have to advertise it."

It was like a punch to the gut. I couldn't say anything.

"Do you know how many people have complained to me about you being so flamboyant? You need to settle the hell down or you are going to lose the few friends you have left."

Dumbfounded, all that came out of my mouth was, "What? Who?"

My dad simply walked off and left me in panicking on the sidewalk. I understood he was actually angry about what was going on in town, but he took it out on me. I started to cry.

A few days later another State Representative held a meeting at the restaurant next to the store. Michele Johnson stood up in front of the packed room filled with residents and suggested Ofiara let a private corporation buy out the utilities department. She felt a business could better manage public funds than the town. Luckily, there was someone there to question the suggestion.

Janice shouted from the back "I don't think that is going to work."

The representative looked incensed "I think it will," she replied. "There are several areas of the world where privatization has been very successful. An example of this would be South Africa."

Janice interrupted the politician. "In South Africa many of those who are close to or under the poverty line end up drinking contaminated water because they cannot afford the prices corporations charge."

My dad was standing with Jill and Eric on the other side of the room. He looked over at me as though I should do something. I shrugged my shoulders back at him. I had no idea what to do.

Michele looked a little irritated. "This is not something I just pulled out of my head. The people I talked with about this are experts from all over the world."

Janice was also getting a little irritated. "I have actually been there and worked in those areas. The poor, those people who have trouble buying food; they are the ones who suffer the most from privatization of water systems. Privatization does not work."

"Government managing a business is never a good idea," Michele responded.

"I would argue that a human need shouldn't be made into a business." Janice did not flinch or miss a beat. "However, if you truly believe this is a move in the best interest of the town and capitalism, I would challenge you to tell me where the competition will be?"

"Sorry?" the congresswoman asked.

Janice smiled and said, "In a free market, businesses compete. That competition offers a chance to produce both the best product and the product which can be purchased for the lowest amount of money. In Ofiara, there is one utilities department. I will admit I'm not an economist. However, it stands to reason that the town is not big enough to offer any sort of competition. Therefore, what it looks like you are proposing is a monopoly on the water supply."

Michele suddenly lit up as though she had the answer. "The water company would be accountable to both local government as well as the people of Ofiara."

Janice licked her lips. "So, what you are proposing is bringing in a private water company to be monitored by the government? It seems like that would be more expensive."

Michele was clearly flustered. "If you would like to talk more about this after the meeting, I can certainly address any questions then, but I think I better continue."

I glanced over at my dad who looked pissed. It was always difficult for him if someone made a valid argument which opposed any idea he felt was good.

The one thing that we figured out quite quickly was monetary and corporate power brings political power. After the meeting, Peter walked over and hugged the congresswoman. He took a step back and proceeded to tell her about how much he respected her family values platform.

Jill and I silently looked on. It was like watching a car accident in slow motion. Danny walked up behind us and made a gagging sound.

Everything offered to us was from some foreign perspective that was not going to benefit the town. The solutions all came from people who did not have to live in town or face the consequences of what Polar had done. Not one of the politicians said anything about the responsibility of Polar Beverage.

Worst of all, in the eyes of some Ofiara residents, these solutions offered hope. The difficulty with hope, at least from my perspective, is that it sometimes works as a wall between the person who feels the hope and their life. Feeling hope makes people stand in the same place, waiting for change. The difficulty is someone waiting for something that may or may not make one happy prevents that person from engaging in the rest of their life, moving on. I was scared that hope, false hope, was going to prevent people in town from looking at other options.

Chapter 42

What ran out of the faucets was down to a trickle. It would take forever to fill a sink or a bathtub. I felt so defeated, as did the other protesters. It felt like fighting a battle which could not be won.

We had even tried to enlist help from the outside. We told the world what had happened in our small town. We had told politicians, Polar shareholders, and then we told the media. We told them how Polar Beverage had monopolized our water supply. Honestly, it didn't make a difference.

Media finally decided to show up towards the end of the June. They took pictures and video. Reporters talked to several people in town; mainly, they talked to local residents who weren't actually involved with the protest but were angry about the water prices. When the story finally aired, what people saw was a group of people protesting water prices. There was nothing said about Polar Beverage and their contribution to the water problems. Moreover, the story was very short-lived in the media, replaced by other more exciting issues.

Larry Bachmann, an anti-gay preacher, was arrested at a rest area just outside Minneapolis. He had allegedly propositioned an undercover officer in an attempt to have sex with another man. This story was much more popular.

The Bachmann scandal also eclipsed another important news item. It was at the bottom of the fourth page. The small article, only a few sentences long, told readers that Franklin Jackson had been cleared of all charges related to Terry finding the ingredients to make meth in his barn.

We continued to walk in circles with our signs. Our hope had dwindled to a mere ember in the fire. We all smelled terrible as the June sun took advantage of the warm humid summer air.

I ducked out for a while and walked over to the store. I needed a breather. Things felt a little on the side of hopeless.

In the giant cooler, I found the leftover cases of Polar Beverage water and soda. Eric's truck was parked in the alley behind the store. Catching my second wind I filled the truck with cases of bottles and cans. I then drove over to the beverage plant. Getting out of the truck, I grabbed a case of water and walked over to the middle of the protesters and, one by one, I opened the water and dumped each bottle onto the dirt road in front of Polar. The others started grabbing water and other products and dumping them then throwing the empty cans and bottles over the Polar fence. When the bottles and cans were gone, a few large men grabbed a few cases of water from a pallet just outside fence of the plant, bringing it to the middle of the road and dumping the bottles out.

I looked up past the fence to some of the workers. They stared with disdain, feeling as though we were the enemy. In their minds it was them against us. We were the evil ones trying to take down their livelihood and prevent their families from eating.

Just then I looked up to see Peter walking towards the fence with Douglas close behind. Douglas watched people dump their water and pop in the street. I saw something in his eyes, not the normal look; rather, this time he had a look of defiance. Douglas felt it; the proof was in the sliver of a grin in the corner of his mouth. I stood up and looked straight in his eyes and grinned back. In my head I was saying, "Do it, just fucking do it, you are so much better than this."

Peter looked at Douglas and motioned for him to walk inside with him, but Douglas was at his end. He took off his name tag and handed it to Peter.

"At one point or another we have to decide that something is not working," Douglas said to Peter.

"Douglas, if the plant goes, this entire town will go down. How can you possibly justify this?" Peter said imploring him.

"I'm actually ok with that," Douglas said with a smile, grabbing Peter and hugging him. Douglas then walked to the entrance of the chain link fence, carefully opened it, and walked through.

Early that evening when the protest had died down, I walked over to see Douglas. He had started a bonfire in a large pit he dug at the end of his yard only a few feet from the lake. He decided to have a party to celebrate what he saw as his new-found freedom.

"So, what are you going to do for a job now?" I asked.

"I am still weighing my possibilities," he said, poking a stick into the fire.

"You could always go back to activism," I responded.

"That part of me is going to be there no matter what." Douglas smiled and put his arm around me. "Thank you," he said and kissed me on the side of the face.

"For what?" I asked.

I looked over to see Danny and Eric walking around the side of the house.

"Some of the first ones here. Wow. And, we are going to be the last ones to leave," Eric said. He wasn't kidding.

Danny was painfully quiet and Eric looked a bit depressed.

"How you two doing?" I asked.

"Yeah," she said with a smile. "I am just feeling a little worn down,"

"Yeah," I said.

"I feel stupid," Danny said sitting on the ground next to the fire. "We didn't make a difference at all."

Eric responded, "And honestly, I'm just really fucking tired."

"It just seems like we suck," Danny said, looking into the fire.

Douglas sat down on the other side of the fire pit. "Years ago I was working with a non-profit. We worked to bring clean water to groups of people who did not have access to the money or resources which would enable them to have something we take for granted. Correction, something we took for granted. People didn't donate a great deal. I think part of it was that people could not conceive of water being an issue. Then, one day we got a very large donation." Douglas pointed at Eric and Danny. "We had no idea who made the donation, but suddenly there was close to a million dollars in the account. We should probably have said something but we decided not to. We used the money to go into villages in all over the world which had high infant death rates due to unclean water. We would ask them if they felt a well would help. If the answer was yes, we would build a well. That money, that risk these individuals took, saved the lives of thousands of people simply by giving them clean drinking water."

Chapter 43

I was a little surprised the Water Carnival happened that year. It was the first summer there would be no water fights. With the lack of water pressure, the decision to use water for fun rather than need could not be justified.

There was also the continued indignity of skyrocketing water prices. The utilities department and the city council both knew there would be a need to drill another well, a deeper well. Ofiara certainly didn't have the funds to pay for additional drilling. The cost to town was adding up and Polar Beverage was not planning on chipping in funds for assistance in this new well.

The good news was that, despite the water shortage, the carnival would go on. And as the weekend continued, it became obvious the same was true for fun. There were vendors selling all sorts of food and trinkets. The lake was filled with boats. Overall, people were enjoying themselves and neglecting their worries.

The second night of Water Carnival the public beach filled with people setting up lawn chairs and picnic blankets. Everyone was talking and mingling between groups. It felt as though that invisible line which divided the town had disappeared.

Jill and I went to the lake very early to get a spot in the middle of the beach and several feet from shore. We set out our patchwork quilt and a cooler filled with beer. There was a breeze coming off the water as the sun reached the edge of the world, close to disappearing for the evening.

I noticed Terry wandering across the beach with some guy. He was tall and much younger than she. He looked as though he had money. It was difficult for me to picture her falling for any guy who didn't have a great deal of money. She looked back and gave a polite wave to me and Jill. Eventually, Terry and her male companion decided to park their blanket about twenty feet from us. I turned my head so that she could not see my lips and whispered to Jill "Oh, she is just evil."

Jason joined us with Monet at his side. He immediately went for the beer cooler.

"I don't think so," I said shutting the plastic cover on his hand.

"I will check back with you in a little while, see if you have changed your mind."

"Yeah," I said to Jason. "You do that."

The next people to join us were Todd and Jake. Jake was in charge of the volunteer fire department, and as such, was wearing a red helmet. I wasn't sure if he actually needed the hard hat or was simply using it as a prop to impress and pick up women.

Todd on the other hand looked tired. He was still bartending part-time and hadn't found a full-time job. He was at a point where he was scared he might lose his house. About 80% of his life savings had been spent on house and car payments while he was in jail. Todd simply looked defeated. He sat in the sand rather than on the blanket, staring off into the distance and pushing the sand back and forth with his feet.

John came up from behind us yelling loudly, "Hello ladies!"

"Hello Father," said Jill loudly, a smile on her face.

John immediately grabbed a beer without asking. He was dressed grungy with flannel and ripped jeans.

"Today has been a long day and I thank you for the beer," John said right before drinking half his bottle.

I looked over at Terry, who was looking backwards but not at me. She was looking at John. John was looking at the lake, and it seemed as if he was purposely trying not to look at Terry and her guy just feet from us. Perhaps I was reading too much into it.

"When are those pesky fireworks going to start?" I asked, trying to start a conversation.

Jake responded sarcastically, "The same time they do every year Sarah, at dusk."

"What the hell is dusk really?" asked Jill, taking a long drink of beer.

"When it gets dark," said Jake.

The man Terry had been with all evening started walking towards the road, most likely to get her makeup case. She stood up, taking a look at us and at John, mainly at John. I leaned over to Jill and whispered, "Shit."

Jill responded with "Yes, shit indeed."

Terry started to walk over with the movements of a pin-up girl. It seemed like she would use any and all excuses to be close to him. I don't think she understood how much damage she had caused to the lives of so many people in town and there was no sign of things getting better.

"How is everyone tonight?" Terry asked with her lip gloss smile.

"Fine," I said, but I was quickly interrupted by John.

"We're doing as well as can be expected when unseen forces are fucking with our world." He looked directly at her with the deathly stare.

"You know, none of this is my fault," Terry responded defensively.

"Oh, I believe you." John said calmly. "Terry, you may not have been the one who sucked our water supply dry or economically devastated our town but you are supporting the ones who do."

"What are you implying?" Terry asked.

"I'm not implying, Terry." John responded.

Jill interrupted. "We're having a nice time," she smiled at Terry. "I think you should leave Terry."

There was a cold silence for what seemed like several seconds.

"OK then," smiled Todd, seemingly waking from his emotional coma.

John continued to sit there, anger and bitterness shooting from his eyes.

"Terry you little tart, are you flirting with Jill again?" said a voice from behind.

I turned to see the welcome surprise of Douglas, arm in arm with Heidi. I silently hoped this meant they had come to some sort of a solution or agreement, perhaps because Douglas had finally quit the plant.

"Sorry? What?" Terry asked defensively.

"I would like to enjoy my evening, with my girl," Douglas said looking at Heidi. "And I would like to do so with my friends."

"Ok?" Terry said, squinting a little at Douglas.

"I am very politely asking you to leave," Douglas said, without even flinching as if he was asking for a pack of gum at the store.

"Oh," she responded, rolling her eyes but not moving.

"Go now please," Douglas said in a firm voice.

Terry turned around and started walking away. "Bye John," she said.

When she said this, John got up "I will be back in a while, but for now I have to cool down."

"I have to go as well, you cool cats and kittens," Jake said. "I have to supervise the guy who is running the fireworks show." He smiled. "This show is not for us though, it is for Jacqueline."

Although the city was running low on money, the resorts were able to get together and pay half of the cost of the fireworks. Unfortunately, Ofiara still had to go with a pyrotechnic company which didn't have the best of reputations, but did have great prices. In other words, we knew it would be an awesome show created by someone who was not a hundred percent sure of what he was doing.

I knew enough to leave John alone. It didn't seem as though Terry had learned the same lesson. She had followed John down the beach trying to talk to him. Additionally, the guy who had escorted her to the beach returned just in time to see her gently put her hand on John's arm.

"Don't touch me, I am asking you. No, I am begging you, don't do that," John said as he pulled his arm away and walked off. Terry's male friend quickly walked over to comfort her.

The wind had picked up when the fireworks started with a big red white and blue bang. The sky filled with all colors and shapes reflected on the waves of the lake. I looked at Jill and smiled.

John was standing in the shallow water on the beach. Whatever was going on between him and Terry looked to me like a long and painful goodbye. However, in this case, one of the members didn't seem to want to let go. It didn't matter what boundary lines John had drawn over the years or how many times he said it was over, she could see the spark in his eye, and she fed off of it. She knew unequivocally, John was the one man who would always have feelings for her.

Jill looked around. "Does it seem a little too windy for fireworks?"

"Yes," said Heidi, looking at Douglas.

Douglas got up and walked over to where Jake was sitting monitoring the guy shooting off the explosives. Jake stood up and started looking around as though he were searching for something.

"Something isn't right," I said, looking around.

I stood up, followed by Jill, and started walking over to Douglas and Jake.

Suddenly, there was a scream from someplace in the crowed.

Jake darted for the street and then I saw it. There was smoke. It looked like it was coming from the store. I started running and yelling, "Shit, shit, damn it!" with several other people trailing behind me. The fireworks stopped and everyone started moving in the direction of the smoke.

When I reached the store, my out of breath body walked around the front, panting, looking through the glass for a sign of sparks and destruction, but there was nothing. The town's sirens went off indicating that any and all volunteer fire fighters needed to get to the fire station. I ran through the back alley past the back door to the restaurant. I was looking for something to confirm the safety of my store. I finally realized the smoke was not coming from the store. It was billowing out of a still unknown source at least two blocks away. Walking out of the alley, a wall of heat hit me as I looked down the street. The smoke was coming from the Polar Beverage building.

As I walked towards the building the town's fire truck raced past, slowing down and parking at the hydrant in front of the building. One side of the building was engulfed in flames with smoke flowing out of the side windows.

Douglas ran past me, towards the building. He stopped and talked to one man outside then ran to the fire truck and grabbed a helmet.

"What the hell are you doing Douglas?"

"I think Juan is in there, he was working security tonight."

"We'll get him," my dad said putting on a fire jacket. "Stand back Douglas."

Douglas looked calm for what may have been a fraction of a second and then darted towards the building.

"Douglas, damn it!" yelled my dad, running after Douglas who disappeared into the front doors. My dad followed Douglas into the entrance of the building that was billowing smoke.

My dad always said a person could be judged by how they reacted in an emergency situation. A person could plan out as many good deeds as they wanted, but, if they didn't immediately react humanely in a tragedy, he felt there was a major moral flaw in that individual's character. Although I did not agree with this particular measure of humanity, it was clear Douglas indeed passed this test.

"Shit!" I closed my eyes.

Jill's arm moved around me. I could feel anxiety rage through my body.

The other fire fighters arrived as Jake and Eric hooked the hose up to the hydrant. Eric gave the signal to the other firefighters he was turning on the water. He then turned the giant bolt on the side of the hydrant, which resulted in little more than a trickle.

Jake looked over at me in a panic. "Sarah, call Grand Rapids. We need a water truck."

As I called, the fire fighters quickly took the hose off the hydrant and attached it to the fire truck.

"There is no way in hell we are going to have enough water." Eric said to Jake.

Terry arrived, regardless of her suspension she switched immediately into law enforcement mode. She started pushing people back and offering encouraging words about the fire department's ability to take care of what was going on.

I watched the building's entry, crying and holding Jill's hand hard enough to sprain it. I turned to see my mother standing behind me.

"Where is Don?" she asked, worried.

I could feel the look of sickness fall down my face. In a whimper I said "Inside."

"Son of a bitch!" She responded with a mixture of panic and anger.

Just after the words came out of her mouth, three figures emerged from the building covered in black soot. Juan had one arm around Douglas and the other around my dad, and while he looked conscious, his legs were not moving. They gently placed their load on the ground and Douglas sat down next Juan.

My mom gave me a quick affirming rub on the back and walked over to where my dad stood and slapped him hard in the face. In turn, he hugged her while she cried.

"It's a goner," he said to my mom.

I walked behind her and looked over at my dad. "I was scared, Dad."

He managed to give me a half-smile and coughed. I knew this was the closest he was going to come to anything resembling an apology for the outburst he had a few weeks before. He was the type of person who never apologized for anything.

The Grand Rapids Fire Department arrived around ten minutes later with two trucks, as did an ambulance. The paramedics lifted Juan onto a stretcher and placed him in the back of the ambulance.

Peter arrived, barely putting his car in park and running up to Douglas, who was coughing up the soot in his lungs.

"Is Juan OK?" Peter asked frantically.

"Yes," said Douglas mid-cough, leaning over and pointing to the ambulance.

Peter moved quickly to the ambulance. "You're going to get you through this Juan."

"You're a fighter, Juan, you are going to be fine!" yelled Sam from within a large group of onlookers around forty feet from the building.

The fire fighters worked for hours battling the out of control industrial fire. Three more trucks had to be called from neighboring towns. All night long, men and women fought the flames and small explosions. People from town brought food and water to the firefighters. Jason brought some blankets and towels his mother had sent.

At about two in the morning, I noticed water pouring out of the back of the factory, much more than the firefighters were pumping inside. I looked around to see if anyone else noticed. Douglas had noticed and simply shook his head disapprovingly.

Peter helped out where he could, but most of the time he spent pacing and biting his nails. At one point in the evening, Jill had walked over to him motioning me to join us. Peter just started sobbing.

"Peter, I am betting your insurance is going to cover this," I said optimistically.

"No, that is not it," he said, giving me a mournful look. "I made a mistake, a very big mistake." He looked at me with a half-smile. "Because, believe it or not, I make a lot of mistakes. The problem is that if Juan dies, I will not be able to take that mistake back."

There it was, carved in stone, the one thing that Peter would not do. He was not willing to kill another person to achieve his goals. Don't get me wrong, it was good to see some level of empathy come from his direction, but it was such a finite and flawed morality. Hurting people was OK until someone got critically injured or killed.

Douglas walked over to where we were sitting on the edge of the fire truck. Peter looked at Douglas.

"We should have found another way," said Douglas.

Peter got up and pointed towards the burning building. "If we had pulled out of here, it would have caused economic damage, do you understand that? If we had not been here, this town would have been economically devastated."

"They would have found a way," Douglas replied, shaking his head. "You think you have the solution for everything."

"No, I think offering people the chance to make a living and feed their families, to have the things you and I have is not a bad thing; in fact it is a gift."

Chapter 44

As I walked to work, smoke burned my eyes and the smell of industrial chemicals made it more than difficult to breathe. While I looked at the devastation, I realized the most disturbing image was not the building that had been ravaged and hollowed out by flames; rather it was the river of water, several feet wide, pouring from a gaping hole in the side of building and over the grass to the lake.

There were embers still fighting to burn, but merely emitting small puffs of smoke. Residents wandered around the Polar building, surveying the damage. They almost looked like zombies moving through a scene from a post-apocalyptic movie, trying to find their lives again.

I knew I had to open the store that morning even though I didn't want to. I would have preferred to stay in bed all day, perhaps for several days, and just forget what had happened during the fireworks. I wanted things; however flawed they were, to go back to normal.

After the cash in the register was counted out and everything set up, I walked to the window and just watched the street for I have no idea how long. The sun was peeking through the wisps of smoke floating down the streets and up through the sky. It created an effect of showing every single detail of town such as peeling paint and cracks in the sidewalk. Everything just looked ugly.

The front door opened and Jason walked in looking frantic and deprived of sleep. "Have you seen Monet?" he asked.

"No," I responded. "The last time I saw him he was with you last night at the fireworks."

"I looked for him after the fire got under control last night. I cannot find him anywhere." Jason said and walked out of the store.

The missing dog just made things worse. I wondered if he had run away; perhaps it was his time to move on. Maybe in the chaos the previous night, Monet had found a girlfriend. Then, from out of nowhere came a thought: Ester and the bottle of strychnine.

My mom walked into the store.

"Morning, Sarah." she said, looking tired.

"Mom, can you watch the store for a few minutes?" I asked.

"Yes, but after that I am heading over to see if Juan's family needs anything."

I ran out of the store and down the street. John was in front of the church and I motioned him to come with me. Without me saying a word he knew there was something very wrong and followed me.

We ran towards the largest house in town. Reaching the fence of the huge Victorian, we peered over a perfect white picket fence. Close to the back door there was a small bowl with what looked like bits and pieces of raw meat. Monet was laying on a cement walkway which curved around the back of the house. We ran around the side of the fence. Monet was laying there with drops of blood leaking from his nose.

I turned to the house to see Ester walking out the side door.

"What the hell, Ester?" I asked.

"He came into my yard and intruded on my life. It's his fault, not mine," she responded with anger in her voice.

"May God have mercy on your soul, Ester," John said, shaking his head.

"Well," Ester said, with one side of her weather-worn lips wrinkled up. "He was a dog, only a dog. It wasn't like he was human. God gave us that right, we are masters over animals. I was simply following God's will."

"You've got to be kidding!" I said. "What is wrong with your head?"

"Excuse me? You are going to lecture me on morality, you dyke? You are the one going to hell, not me," Ester said moving her hand to her back door.

"Ester, we are caretakers, not owners." John said, picking up Monet and cradling the sheep dog in his arms.

She grimaced as though she was going to vomit. "You are probably a faggot too, and all you priests are gays who like to suck dicks and have things shoved up your asses. I bet you like little boys." She opened the door and started to walk in, but in true Ester form, she had to get one last jab in. "I won't be back to your church, and I won't be donating any more money."

"Ok," John said, carrying Monet in his arms.

I put my hand on John's back while we walked to Jason's house.

"Thank you, John."

John's eyes were slightly glazed over as he looked down at Monet, limp in his arms.

I started to cry. "No matter how mean she can be, I just can't believe she did this."

When we rounded the corner onto Main Street, we saw Jason halfway down the block. Without a word he ran over and John slowly placed Monet in his arms. Jason took the dog from John and sat down on the sidewalk. He ran his fingers through the hair on Monet's head and hugged him.

After several minutes, Jason asked us what had happened. John sat down next to him and told him the story, every painful detail.

"How is it so easy for some people?" Jason said looking at Monet's ear then wiping some of the blood away.

Jason and Ester were on opposing sides of a scale of self-awareness. Ester was the kind of person for which every moment in her life was interpreted inside her head. She would never ask the opinion. Always, she would assume she naturally had all the answers. The meaning of everything that happened to her was contingent on past events. On the other hand, Jason interpreted his world by looking outside of himself. He saw the world around him and believed he knew how he fit into the puzzle of life. Ester only saw her life and what she felt affected her life.

Chapter 45

Help for Ofiara would not be coming from the outside. We had to be our own heroes, because no one else really understood what was happening. How was someone from the outside going to identify with our plight? Most people in the surrounding area would not know what it was like to lose water or see a community divided over a resource we all took for granted.

It may possibly have been the busiest city council meeting in the history of the town. The chairs were quickly filled, leaving at least fifty people standing. Many people brought their children because even the babysitters were there. The lucky individuals were the ones who stood outside, unable to fit into the packed hall which smelled like smoke from the night before.

The temperature was quickly rising as sweat poured off the heads of almost every person in the room. Someone had jarred the opening to the hall creating a slight breeze down the aisle in the middle of the room. The workers from the plant and their families were on one side of the room. And on the other side of the room were the people who were unable to put up with dwindling water levels and elevated water prices. On each side, people were talking and planning out what they would say. Since few of the people there that night had ever been to a city council meeting, it was clear many were unsure of what was going to happen.

It didn't matter which side anyone was on; to a certain degree, everyone in that room felt like a loser. It had become abundantly clear that bringing Polar Beverage in presented more than a few problems. Furthermore, the way the town had dealt with those problems was not good. It was like that unhealthy relationship where two people are enmeshed in one another and each wants something completely different. The factory needed to profit, while the town clearly wanted enough money to do more than merely exist on some sort of life support.

I felt so sorry for my dad that night as he stood at the front talking with four of the council members. I knew he had to keep things together in the face of what could quickly turn into a lynch mob mentality. He looked nervous and kept his eyes towards the ground in an attempt to avoid eye contact with anyone in the room. The other council members looked no less fearful and at least one of them was scoping out the nearest exit.

I scanned the room thinking about heading outside for a moment to cool off before the meeting started. Brian Kirkpatrick was standing next to the back exit. He had returned unceremoniously to town without so much of a word of rumor floating around about his return. He was like a ghost in the room.

My dad and the other council members took a seat at a long table at the front of the room. The meeting was then called to order, creating a fragile silence which seemed to be holding the heat still in the air. Everyone knew what was coming. I looked around seeing some angry faces and some with fear. What little glue held the town together had weakened to the breaking point.

Jill looked over at me, fanning her face with a piece of paper. "Oh for fuck's sake, it's hot in here," she whispered.

"Hotter than hell," I whispered back.

John, who was standing ahead of us, turned and nodded in agreement while letting out a sigh.

Eric was watching our dad with a worried look.

My dad spoke. "I am not going to beat around the bush and there will be no minor business tonight. As everyone may have guessed, we have a problem. Right now we have to look at our options and figure out what we are going to do. I am going to first give Peter from Polar Beverage a chance to speak."

There were a few mutters from both sides of the room while Peter walked to the podium.

It was clear his confidence was dwindling. His white shirt was soaked to the point one could clearly see his t-shirt underneath.

"Well," he said, taking a slow look around the room, perhaps looking for allies or adversaries, "we have quite the conundrum."

"Ah, yeah," said a man's voice from the crowd, which was echoed with agreement by several people.

"We want to know what we are going to do!" yelled a woman's voice.

Peter continued to maintain an authoritative tone in his voice. "Polar Beverage is looking at different options for what is going to be done with the plant." Peter paused for a moment and looked around again. "The first option we are looking at is rebuilding the plant at its current location."

Peter's statement was met with a handful of loud jeers which quickly escalated from both sides of the room. Both sides started shouting all sorts of cruel and negative things at one another, at their neighbors.

"Ok, ok," my dad said. Frustrated, he shouted, "OK. That is quite enough! Settle the hell down, God damn it!"

The noise in the room again became tolerable.

I felt water dripping down my back.

Peter waved both hands up and down several times trying to calm the people down. After several minutes, the room started to quiet down, giving Peter a window to speak again. "Another option would be for Polar Beverage to try and rebuild a few blocks away from the original site and further away from Main Street."

There were sighs and moans, made worse by the temperature, which seemed to be increasing by the second.

My dad stood up and yelled, "Just let him finish!" He looked over at Peter, "Please continue."

"You know, there is always the option of Polar Beverage simply collecting the insurance money and leaving town," Peter said coldly. He peered from one side of the room to the other, looking to see the effectiveness of his threat.

I looked over at Douglas, who shook his head and whispered, "There is no way the insurance company is going to give out that money. The reason the building was so badly burned was because Polar had monopolized the water system. Peter is going to have to figure out a way to make this look either like an act of vandalism or a freak accident."

"Does Peter know that?" I asked

Douglas replied, "I am sure he does. He also knows that if Polar Beverage is going to set up another plant, he has to have the people begging for it."

"We don't want Polar using all of the town's water until we are dry," shouted a woman in the crowd. After a moment, I realized it was Danny's voice.

Others in the crowd started to join in, trying to get their side of the argument heard. Above the mutters and chaos, came a woman's voice, although most people couldn't hear what she was saying. Her words only became clear at the tail end of her statement. "If you hadn't let this company build here, nothing would have happened to the water. We are now worse off than when Polar came in."

"Fuck you! You are nothing but a white trash whore. Go back to the trailer park and have another baby!" a male voice yelled in response.

The last comment fuelled a few more minutes of yelling, each side trying to violently express what they were trying to say. All sorts of language, some of which I had never heard, was exchanged. Some individuals were waving their arms around, perhaps in an attempt to make the other side understand. It was clear words were not working.

My father stood up and yelled, "Hey, we need to calm the hell down!" He continued to yell for a few minutes and then finally snapped. He grabbed his chair and started slamming it violently against the floor, "Quiet down now!" He may as well have been speaking Latin. Not one person was listening.

John had just about reached his breaking point. He pushed his way through the crowded room. When he finally reached the front, he yelled, "Shut the hell up, shut up now!"

Everyone quieted down, except one woman who was finishing her point with tears running down her face. "How the hell am I supposed to feed my children when I cannot even afford water?"

Another voice yelled, "Get a job, you dumb bitch!"

"I have a job asshole," she responded.

John started yelling at the top of his lungs, "Shut up now! All of you! Why are you even bothering?" The room started to quiet down. "No one is listening!" He pointed around the room. "These are your neighbors, your friends, and your family! Do none of you feel you have any vested interest in knowing what they are going through? All I'm hearing people say is me, me, me!"

There were a few mutters from the audience and then my dad spoke, waving his finger at the participants in the audience. "No! You don't get to do this! How many of you have actually attended a city council meeting in the last year?" He paused and looked around. "Go ahead, please, and raise your hands."

A few people scattered across the room raised their hands.

"You know what? I know the number without actually having anyone tell me. The number is twelve. Of all of those who have attended the meetings, the highest number of individuals we have had stay through the entire meeting has been twelve, and that only happened twice. In the last year, I would have welcomed the presence of members of the community. It would have been nice to have someone there, someone with the answers, but this is just pissing and moaning." My dad paused, then let the final bomb go, "You don't get to completely just drop out of the political process and then have the audacity to come back after the meeting is over and criticize what we are doing. It does not work that way!"

My dad paused, then took a deep breath, "OK, if anyone has anything constructive to say we can start the meeting again." He sat down and sighed.

Suddenly, the earth shook and there was a loud crash. It sounded as if someone was dropping semi-trucks or a plane had crashed into the middle of town. The entire building went completely silent as everyone looked over at one another. The noise then repeated itself two more times.

Several people in the room started whispering as though being too noisy would bring on the sound again. Slowly, people started standing, unsure of the ground. I realized I had been holding onto Jill.

When we finally got outside, I could see dust floating and pushing between the homes and buildings. I followed John through a thick cloud of particles and debris floating around us. After several minutes, the air started to clear. People started to chatter a bit then grew silent again. People just stared, frozen and unclear about what had happened. The Polar Beverage building was gone, not just a little, it had just disappeared completely.

Peter slowly walked over to where his multi-million dollar complex stood and put his hands on his head, quickly running his fingers through his hair. He was followed by other townspeople, who just stood at the edge for several minutes looking on in shock and surprise. The remnants of the building and its contents were at the bottom of a giant sink-hole the size of a city block.

It was karma, pure and simple. Peter and the others had asked too much of the land.

Peter was standing at the edge of the hole, which looked to be almost a hundred feet deep. "Was there anyone in the building?" No one was responding, so Peter yelled again, "For Christ sake! Hello, was there anyone in the building?"

Everyone looked around. No one seemed to notice anyone missing.

John walked over and placed his hand on Peter's shoulder.

Peter turned to John and asked "Do you still think that this was man's work and not God? I think God clearly told us something tonight."

"No Peter, still not God."

www.ingramcontent.com/pod-product-compliance
Lightning Source LLC
Chambersburg PA
CBHW081149170626
46813CB00009B/3126